For Justice or Love

SULLIVAN FAMILY BOOK 2

Milan Watson

TABLE OF CONTENTS

For Justice or Love

Book 2 in the Sullivan Family Series,
filled with danger, deceit and desire

When a female firefighter rescues a state prosecutor in the middle of the night the heat is about to rise...

After fleeing an abusive relationship, Delta Eckhart plans on starting a new life in a new town. Her only plan is to heal her heart along with her bruises.

Neal Sullivan is a prosecutor for the State of Delaware. He has committed his life to pursuing justice, albeit with a perpetual frown and an aversion to relationships.

When Delta rescues Neal from a broken elevator, the attraction is instant but both deny it. The heat imminently rises when they discover they are neighbors.

Will Delta be able the heal the wounds of an abusive relationship and open her heart to love again? Can Neal learn that there is a place for love in his life along with the pursuit of justice? Will justice or love prevail?

For Justice of Love is a tale of heartbreak and new beginnings. This is Book 2 in the Sullivan Family Series although it can be read as a standalone novel.

For Lucas and Alexander

"…and she loved a little boy
very very much,
even more than
she loved herself."
~ *Shel Silverstein*

Also by Milan Watson

Seduced by the Boss

A Stranger Like You (a short story)

Sullivan Family Series

Bride on the Run (Book 1)

For Justice or Love (Book 2)

WOULD YOU LIKE A FREE BOOK?

Simply sign up for the Milan Watson Newsletter on her website at

www.milanwatson.com

You can follow her page on Facebook for new releases:

https://www.facebook.com/MilanWatsonAuthor

PROLOGUE

SHE WOKE TO the metallic taste of blood. Even after she swallowed a few times, the taste remained. Tentatively, she ran her fingers over her skull, where the pain throbbed in time with her heartbeat.

The bump wasn't bleeding, but it was big. The size of a ping pong ball, would be her best guess.

The slightest move caught her breath as a sharp pain shot through her chest. It felt as if a white-hot knife had just sliced through her abdomen.

Lying back, her one eye fluttered closed as she clung to her consciousness.

She mentally did an inventory of her injuries. There was the ping pong ball knob on her head – one. One eye wouldn't open, it was swollen shut - two.

Her tongue glided along her lips, and she tasted more blood. That would explain the metallic taste in her mouth – three.

Running a hand over her torso, she ascertained that the stabbing pain was coming from the right side of her ribcage, probably broken or at least cracked– four.

Her toes and feet responded when she moved them; no injury there. She could lift both her legs. Good, her legs were working. Now if only she could get past the pain, she could get out of here.

Four.

That was four injuries too many. Delta Eckhart closed her eye, the one that wasn't already swollen shut, and made herself a promise. She wasn't going to be a victim any longer.

Gathering all her courage and scraping together the last scraps of her strength, she pushed up from the floor, ignoring the shooting bolt of pain as her body resisted. As soon as she was in a sitting position, she noticed Craig through the darkness. He was fast asleep, snoring on the couch. She still struggled to wrap her mind around it. The man she had fallen in love with, that she had dreamed of growing old with, had done this to her. After two years, his true colors finally waved their flag. She pinched back the tears that threatened to fall.

If she wanted to survive, she needed to get out.

She slowly dragged herself across the floor to the bedroom. If she made a single sound, Craig could wake up, and this time she wasn't sure he would stop when she was down.

She bumped into a lamp, her breath caught and the world spun as she reached; luckily she caught it just before it crashed on the floor. She quietly placed it on the floor and continued dragging herself further. She didn't even have the liberty to cry out from the pain. Her breath was coming in short, painful pants; the exertion and the throbbing pain in her chest made breathing even harder.

Delta pushed through the fuzziness that had settled over her brain like a cobweb and continued to painfully alternate shuffling and slithering to the bedroom.

She could do this.

If she could run into a building as it was being consumed by a ravenous fire, she could sure as hell crawl out of an abusive relationship.

Slowly, she crossed the threshold into their bedroom and instantly felt guilty for bleeding on the beautiful beige carpet. She had saved over six months for the luxurious carpet and had only managed to have it installed the week before.

She shook her head. How twisted could guilt get? *Ouch!* No sudden movements, she chastened herself. It wasn't her fault that she was bloody and crawling; she refused to feel guilty about the damn carpet.

As Delta slowly pulled herself up against the bed, the red-hot sting of pain shooting through her body with fresh enthusiasm made her light-headed.

Closing her good eye, she took a minute to steady herself before she slowly walked to the bathroom, her body protesting with every step.

Her reflection caused a tear to slip down her cheek. She brushed it away furiously as she studied Craig's latest handiwork. Her eye was already purple and swollen shut; her top lip had a nasty cut that was still oozing blood.

She quietly pulled the bathroom door closed and opened the tap. The cold wash cloth she dabbed against her eye and lip bought the stinging pain down to a throb.

As she caught her reflection for the second time, her eyes drew together as the question crossed her mind. *When did she become a victim of physical abuse?*

Her good eye narrowed with anger as she cleaned the blood

off her face. Determined to get out before Craig woke up, she strode into the bedroom, grabbed a large gym bag, and started stuffing in a few items of clothing and some personal things. When the bag couldn't take anymore and Delta knew she wouldn't be able to carry more, she zipped it shut, accepting that she would be leaving the rest of her things, of her life, behind.

She grabbed concealer from the dresser and started applying it generously. She surveyed her battered appearance in the mirror; it looked terrifying, but only if you looked closely. She snatched a ball cap from the cupboard and placed it low over her face. Better. She looked at her bedroom of two years for the last time before picking up the gym bag.

Her body flinched at the effort, but Delta pushed through the pain and found her courage and finally her anger. Clenching her jaw, she softly walked past Craig snoring on the couch, and out the front door.

Delta watched the apartment door in fear as the elevator doors closed. If Craig caught her now…

When the doors finally closed and the elevator started to descend, she took a deep breath for the first time. When she flinched at the pain, the woman beside her looked at her curiously.

Delta bent her head, focusing on the floor. She hunched down, covering her swollen eye with a loose strand of hair. Best not to draw attention; she needed to get as far away from Craig as possible before he woke up.

She stepped into the rain, thankful that the nearest bus station was only a few blocks away. She forced herself to put one foot in front of the other until she reached it.

Winter had just dug its icy claws into the city; the wind slapped her face every step of the way. Delta reached the bus station, exhausted and aching. Luckily, the first bus pulled up a couple of minutes later.

Noticing Delta's struggle to walk, the bus driver narrowed his eyes as she climbed into the bus.

"You taking the bus, lady?" He was an old man with a scarred face, but the kindness in his eyes made Delta answer honestly.

"I just need to get away…as far as possible." She panted at the effort of speaking.

The old man leaned down and noticed the cracked lip and swollen eye. He knew a runner when he saw one, and this one had to run fast and hard. "East Coast far enough for you?"

Delta tried to smile, but her lip pulled, and she felt a fresh drop of blood leak into her mouth. Grabbing a tissue from her pocket, she dabbed at it. "Definitely."

The bus driver nodded and took her gym bag, "Well, come on. The bus isn't that full tonight; you can have the back seat and try to sleep a bit."

"I don't –" Delta stammered. "I don't have a ticket."

"You got money?" he asked honestly.

"Yes." Delta mentally calculated the cash in her purse.

"Fine, you get on the bus, and we'll sort it out in the morning."

"Thank you." Delta slowly moved to the back of the bus.

As soon as she was settled in the backseat and the bus started to move, Delta dug in her bag for the pain tablets she had thrown in as an afterthought. She swallowed them without water and lay back against the grey fabric seat. Shivering and sore, she closed her eyes and refused to let the tears fall. She wasn't going to cry for a man that could tell her he loved her and then beat her.

The bus pulled out and made its way to the highway, lulling her to sleep as she moved further and further away from the man she had loved and had now come to hate.

Chapter 1

Six Months Later...

AFTER A LONG day of arguing with the opposing counsel, Neal Sullivan wanted nothing more than a cold beer and the comfort of his couch.

He placed his case files in his briefcase, vowing not to look at them tonight, but he already knew that he would. He always did.

Some lawyers did it for the money; Neal did it for justice. It wasn't simply a job to him; it was his vocation. Being a prosecutor had always been his dream. He spent every waking hour working on cases or reviewing them. His family often said he needed to get a life, but for Neal, there was nothing wrong with the one he had.

He enjoyed his work, the satisfaction of putting a perpetrator behind bars. The long hours and hard work were part of the deal. It didn't bother him. Yes, it might be nice to go out after a long day for a couple of beers with friends, but his brothers were his friends.

Friends expected too much; they expected unplanned drinks and weekends spent together. Although he was single, Neal didn't feel like going out every night.

He didn't enjoy idle chitchat about sports when he was working towards putting a rapist behind bars.

Whenever a case started to get to him or he needed to unload the heavy weight a state prosecutor carried, he would visit his parents. His mother always had a way to calm him, and his father always had sound advice. The few times he didn't have advice, he was a patient sounding board.

Even as a child, Neal had enjoyed solitude over birthday parties, his books over conversation. Few people understood him, although most respected and admired his work ethic.

He had never been very social and had never felt inclined to have a large group of friends. He had everything he needed.

If and when he needed the warmth and comfort of a woman, he would get it, but there wouldn't be any second dates. He didn't have time or the inclination for another relationship. His only two relationships had burned him. With the first, he was young and in love until he discovered she was sleeping with the opposing counsel. When his second relationship also ended with infidelity, Neal decided he had had enough of women and their cheating ways.

He shrugged on his coat and walked towards the elevators. Being a prosecutor for the State of Delaware, he often found himself alone in the office late at night.

With large sums of money and partnerships being dangled in front of them like carrots, corporate lawyers were motivated to work late. When you worked for the state, however, your only incentive was justice. And that didn't incentivize all Neal's colleagues to work until eleven on a Tuesday night. He headed towards the ancient elevator and pressed the down button, glancing at his watch. It was going on quarter past eleven. It would be too late to grab supper from the health bar on the way to his apartment; he'd have to settle for pizza tonight, again.

The elevator pinged, and the doors opened. He stepped inside, thinking about the toppings he would like tonight, going through the same ritual he always did. He'd think about trying olives or Parmesan or maybe even living on the wild side and adding some chilies, but his order always remained the same: pepperoni, cheese, and pineapple. It wasn't that he was afraid to try something new. He was just comfortable with what he knew, and he liked it. Where was the harm in ordering something you knew you were going to enjoy?

Thud!

Neal's briefcase bounced on the elevator floor as it came to an abrupt stop between the sixth and seventh floor. Great! This was just what he needed: being stuck in an ancient elevator in the middle of the night. His stomach growled, realizing the pizza would be postponed. He pulled out his cellphone to call the super, but the signal bar taunted him with zero reception. Seeing no other way out, he pressed the emergency button on the panel board. Within a few seconds, a female operator promised him that the fire department would be on its way shortly.

Neal sat down on the elevator floor, knowing that the dirt and grime would probably ruin his best suit, and waited for the fire department. He hated the smell of elevators. They always smelled musty and faintly of lemon disinfectant.

Bored senseless thirty minutes later, he contemplated taking out his case files, but he knew he wouldn't be able to focus while sitting in a stuck elevator. He looked at the brass railing against the side of the elevator and wondered when someone had last thought to polish, or preferably disinfect, them?

A short while later he heard voices outside the elevator, the intercom came on, and a man promised they'd be right up. He felt the elevator drop a few inches and berated himself when his heart jumped into his throat.

There was nothing like a little loss of control to put your nerves on edge, he thought as he stood up and grabbed onto the railing, just before the elevator dropped a few inches again. His heart was thundering in his ears. He tried to calm himself; *they know what they are doing*, he tried to placate himself.

He heard a scratching sound at the door just before the tip of a red crowbar peeked through.

"Hey, can you hear me?" came a female voice.

"Yeah, just get me out of this thing before I plummet to the basement." Neal hated the nervous tone of his own voice.

The female voice laughed as the crowbar reached deeper into the elevator, prying the doors open. "You just settle down, I've almost got it."

When the doors opened, Neal realized the elevator had stopped just below the seventh floor. He could see the roof of the sixth floor through the small gap in the elevator doors.

A female firefighter, perched on a ladder, stood peeking through the gap. "Come on, you'll need to crawl out of this space, but we don't want to risk lowering this old girl any further. She might make a run for it." Even with her helmet and safety gear, her smile was attractive.

Neal looked out of the small space and noticed the elevator floor was about fifteen inches below the roof of the sixth floor. He pushed his briefcase at her before lying down, readying himself for the crawl. Once the briefcase was safely out of sight, he slowly crawled towards her; her smile was childlike and soothing. He focused on that and not the fact that if the elevator should fall or climb at this minute, he'd be split in half.

He was about halfway through when he heard a menacing screeching sound coming from the bowels of the elevator. In a split second, the female firefighter grabbed his arms and tugged hard. Hard enough to have him flying through the small opening just in time when the elevator dropped to the basement. He fell on top of her, the ladder crashing down beside them.

"Are you all right?" he asked, searching her eyes for pain or injury, but he only found humor.

"I'm fine, big boy, but you might want to get off so I can catch my breath." Her smile was wide, her eyes the green of a stormy ocean. For a moment, he felt lost in them; they drew him in like a siren on the open sea.

She was soft beneath him, and even through the thick fire retardant suit, he could feel her body tense. He couldn't help but smile at her. "Never thought I'd be saved by a girl." His voice was soft and taunting and sounded foreign even to him.

Delta looked into the blue eyes of the man currently pinning her to the floor. It should have been uncomfortable and suffocating, but she found she strangely enjoyed the weight of him pinning her to the floor. His eyes were serious, and yet he had surprised her with a witty comment. She allowed her eyes to roam over his face. He had a strong jaw line and his hair was a dusty blond, cropped short. Knowing she had the eyes of her whole crew on her, she whispered to him, "If you don't get up pretty soon, this girl's going to kick your butt."

Neal laughed as he stood up and took her hand, helping her up. "Thanks anyway."

"Part of the job." Delta eyed him. "If you don't plan on needing our services anymore, we'll be on our way." She turned and had started to get the ladder when another firefighter stopped her.

"You took a nasty fall there, Dee. Let me get the ladder."

"Thanks, Mike," she said before she turned around to look at Neal for the last time. "Maybe you should try and avoid elevators for the rest of the night."

Neal laughed easily, a foreign feeling to him. "I think that would be wise." Neal watched her disappear around the corner while another firefighter stuck an out-of-order sign on the elevator. She was tall and athletically built. He saw a few blonde curls escaping under her headgear and wondered what she would look like without the monstrosity of her fire retardant suit. Confused by the instant attraction he had felt and intrigued by the fact that she was a female firefighter, Neal couldn't help but wonder if he would see her again. *That would be an interesting story, one I wouldn't mind hearing over a glass of wine*, he thought as he brushed off his suit and headed for the stairs himself. Maybe he should try the olives and Parmesan on his pizza after all.

Chapter 2

DELTA RODE BACK to the firehouse, lost in her own thoughts. She was confused by her reaction to the victim.

She could swear it was excitement that had coursed through her veins as he smiled into her eyes. What irritated her even more than the frisson of excitement was that she could still clearly recall he had a boxer's build and piercing blue eyes. The suit, probably designer if she had to guess, fitted him perfectly. Even after being stuck in an elevator, he still looked perfectly groomed. His tie wasn't even tugged loose.

She could try to deny it, but she had just experienced a very real attraction to the elevator victim. An attraction which both scared and fascinated her.

Ever since she boarded that bus six months ago in Chicago, she had avoided all men on a personal level. Unfortunately, due to the scarcity of female firefighters, she couldn't avoid them at work.

The memories of Craig's fists still haunted her; many nights she would wake up sweating and shaking. The nightmares varied, but they all featured Craig. Either he found her and beat her again or she was back in that apartment crawling away from him, but in her dreams, he woke up …

She had gone over and over their whole relationship in her mind, wondering how she didn't see him for what he truly was, and yet there were still no signs that could have warned her.

He was charming, well-spoken, attractive, and had an edge to him that Delta had found very appealing. She had fallen in love rapidly and deeply.

For two years, she had shared her life and her apartment with him. The few times he verbally lashed out at her, Delta had convinced herself it was because his job as a lawyer was stressful.

The first time his fists met her cheek, he had beaten it into her that she shouldn't anger him over small stuff when he got home. He didn't need a nagging girl at home, and he sure as hell didn't need her.

Like all victims, Delta had believed she was to blame and had begun to tread more carefully.

The second time he punched her, Delta ran out of the apartment straight to the police station, but Craig's influence as a top defense attorney in Chicago reached further than she had imagined.

She had waited for two weeks for the police to arrest Craig, but it never happened. Another week later, she received a formal phone call saying the paperwork for her complaint had been misplaced. The police officer requested her to come in to refile the complaint. She knew it would be of no use since the bruises had healed.

Delta had had no choice but to leave it at that; with nowhere else to go, she accepted the blame again and promised herself she wouldn't let him touch her for a third time.

For months following his assault, Craig had spoiled her with exorbitant gifts and flowers, declaring his undying love for her; he even went so far as to sign up for anger management lessons.

The third time had been the most brutal and the last.

Delta pushed the horrible memory of that night into the furthest, darkest depths of her mind; she was on call, and she wouldn't allow Craig to influence her job.

Summoning her best smile, she sat quietly listening to the

crew teasing each other and telling jokes as they made their way back to the firehouse.

Delta stepped into her new apartment the following morning, returning from her shift. She had only moved into the old Victorian apartment building a few days before and hadn't met any neighbors yet.

For the past six months, she had stayed in a different motel every month for the fear of Craig finding her. She had never been more grateful that she hadn't told Craig about her private savings account. The one she had used to save for their wedding. Delta had planned it as a surprise for when they got engaged, a surprise that now allowed her to start a new life in a new town.

Now that she knew the wedding wasn't going to happen, she had decided a couple of weeks ago it was time to find something more permanent. She had viewed quite a few apartments and condos but instantly fell in love with the old Victorian building. After paying the deposit and purchasing a few essential furnishings from second hand stores, she still had money left over. She now thought of that account as her running money and didn't plan on using another cent.

She locked the double locks behind her, placed her bag on the counter, and grabbed an iced tea from the fridge. She loved this time of morning, when she came home from a shift with the next forty-eight hours free, and everyone else was rushing out to their nine to five jobs.

Out of habit, she checked that all the windows were locked. She knew she was safe here, but the fear of Craig finding and hurting her again had awakened a paranoid gene she wasn't even aware she had.

She knew his pride would've been hurt when she had disappeared. If he found her now, Delta was sure he wouldn't stop when she was on the floor.

Knowing she wouldn't get any sleep while these memories flooded her mind, she decided to take a walk in the chilly Wilmington morning to help clear her mind.

She stepped out into the fresh chill and watched parents hurrying their children to school and nine-to-fivers rushing to work. As she meandered along sidewalks, Delta thought back to how she had escaped Chicago and made her way to Wilmington.

She had slept through the whole bus trip; the driver had woken her once they stopped in Boston. The city had been beautiful, but still Delta had wanted to put more distance between herself and Chicago. So she had settled her ticket and stayed on the bus until it reached Wilmington.

Feeling battered and drained, Delta had desperately yearned for a hot bath, a warm meal, and clean clothes. After spending four nights in a motel crying and sleeping, she had decided to find out about the firehouses in Wilmington. Luckily for her, there was one with an immediate opening.

She had called her old chief and, after assuring him she hadn't dropped off the face of the earth, she had asked for an immediate transfer due to personal problems. Because she had proved herself in his house for the past six years, he gave her a great reference, and she was appointed within days.

She failed the initial medical, which indicated she had three cracked ribs, but she promised the chief she would be ready for work within a month.

After hiding out for the greater part of her first month in Wilmington, she eventually convinced herself to join a support group for abused woman. There, she not only found friends, but like-minded strong women who had become victims of domestic abuse.

Her first day in the new firehouse, Delta feared awkward questions, but luckily, her new chief didn't ask too many questions about her reported injuries

A burly man who had been chief over thirty years, Chief Ramsey ran his firehouse with a ruthless hand and kind eyes. Delta respected him from the first day she met him. During her first shift, she could see the crew would be a bit harder.

It had taken her years to prove her worth as a female firefighter in Chicago, and she had a feeling she would be fighting the same battle in Wilmington. Delta was the first woman on their crew, and that didn't make for a friendly welcome.

She had to prove herself over and over again to demonstrate to them that she would be a good contribution to their unit. It was the need to establish herself that had her on the ladder last night, and not one of her crew.

With every call, she volunteered for the most dangerous jobs, not because she was looking for trouble, but to prove to her male team members that she was just as capable. She knew they wouldn't admit it outright, but she had started to recognize respect in their eyes whenever they headed back after a call.

Her feet slapped against the asphalt as she turned around and headed back to the apartment. The chilly fall breeze had ruffled her hair and turned her cheeks rosy. A man in a suit rushed past her, and Delta found herself turning around to see if it was the same man she had rescued last night.

Silly! What were the chances? In a city filled with thousands of suit-wearing men, what were the chances of her meeting the one she saved again?

As she turned back towards the direction of her apartment, she thought back to the night before.

She had tried all night but could no longer deny the attraction she had felt. Those cobalt blue eyes had looked at her as if he was looking into her soul.

Ever since she had left Chicago, whenever a man entered her personal space, fear would clutch at her throat and weaken her knees. The only time the fear didn't take over was when she was on shift.

And yet when Mr. Suit had all but dived onto her last night, it wasn't fear that Delta had experienced. It had been something stronger, more elemental. Something Delta hadn't expected to ever feel again.

When Delta had joined a women's abuse group shortly after arriving in Wilmington, one of the women had suggested she go on a man fast. Very simply put, it meant that for twelve months Delta shouldn't worry about men. No dates, no flirting, no sex. She should allow herself time to heal.

She was into month six of her man fast, and the attraction she had felt last night shocked her.

After crawling out of her apartment, bloodied and beaten, she didn't expect to ever be attracted to another man again. As a taxi zoomed by her, splashing her with water, Delta smiled; maybe she was starting to heal after all. As she stepped back into the old Victorian building, Delta felt lighter and looked forward to much needed sleep and a clearer mind.

Chapter 3

NEAL GULPED DOWN the scalding hot coffee as he grabbed his briefcase. He didn't get much sleep last night, but that was probably normal after a near-death experience with an elevator.

All right, he admitted, *it wasn't near death but it wasn't fun either*. Except for the firefighter. Falling on top of her wasn't exactly what Neal would call unpleasant. Neal could still vividly see her green eyes watching him. He'd need to find out which firehouse she worked at; he'd like to send her flowers to thank her.

He had been amazed by the strong attraction he had felt for her; even with her fire retardant suit, she had sent his blood racing through his veins. Deep down he knew it was probably called something like hero-worship syndrome, and even knowing that, he couldn't stop thinking about her.

He had a few hours before he needed to be in court but wanted to stop by the office early. Grabbing his trench coat, he opened the door and walked out into the hall.

Bam!

He didn't immediately recognize her; she was cursing and collecting all the items that had spilled from her bag that had been knocked onto the floor. Neal bent down to help her; when she looked up, he recognized the green eyes. "You're the firefighter?" He smiled as he picked up a brush and handed it to her.

"Are you?" Neal asked again. He narrowed his eyes and leaned closer.

Delta stepped back, leaning against her door. "Yes, I am."

Neal noticed Delta's eyes dart to him and back into the apartment.

"I'm Neal Sullivan, the guy you saved last night." Neal smiled and pointed to the door against which Delta was standing. "You live there?"

Delta turned and quickly glanced at the door. "Yes, I do."

"Looks like we're neighbors." Neal realized it wasn't surprise but fear shining in her eyes. She looked absolutely petrified. He didn't mean to frighten or scare her; he was just being friendly. He had to admit he was curious about the woman that saved him. "Are you all right? Sorry, I didn't catch your name?"

"It's Delta, and I'm fine. Goodbye." Delta swiftly unlocked her door and ducked inside.

Neal could hear her locking all three locks behind her before Neal could follow or say goodbye.

Neal shook his head as he walked towards the elevator. It only took him a minute to opt for the stairs instead.

Neal liked a puzzle, and Delta was a puzzle, he thought as he started jogging down the stairs.

She was a strong woman, she had to be in order to be a firefighter, and yet he had seen fear in her eyes when he had stepped closer.

He hadn't seen that fear last night when he had found himself crushing her to the floor; he had seen something different then. Something leaning more towards desire than fear. He took the stairs two at a time, checking the time on his watch. He'd still have enough time to go by the office before he headed to court.

His thoughts didn't stay on work for very long; as soon as the cool morning breeze met him outside, he thought of Delta, who had just come in.

Neal wondered if she had just been out jogging or if she just came off shift. He had noticed her cheeks were flushed red, but that could've just been the bite in the air. She wasn't wearing her firefighter's attire, and Neal couldn't help but appreciate every inch of her in her close-fitting sweat suit.

She was taller than he expected, almost the same height as he was. Neal couldn't tell much from her clothes, but she didn't seem overly muscular. He'd bet money on the fact that she'd be well-toned.

He felt the familiar flicker of interest rush through him again. Was he really attracted to his firefighter neighbor?

Since he had avoided dating at all cost for the past few years, his attraction to her intrigued him. No one needed to get burned a third time to realize the oven was hot.

But there was something about Delta that made him want to dip his toes in the dating water again. He would be interested to find out how a girl went about becoming a firefighter; was their training the same as the men's? Was the job expectation the same?

And most of all, he wondered what had put the fear behind her beautiful green eyes when he recognized her this morning.

Pushing thoughts of Delta aside, he started running through a case in his head. Time to put his head back in the game.

The elevator doors pinged open, and Neal breathed for the first time since getting in. He had spent all day in the courthouse taking the stairs up and down from his office to court, and his legs were feeling it.

It was stupid, and he'd never been afraid of facing his fears. So when he had walked into the apartment building this evening, he turned stubbornly away from the stairs and headed for the elevator.

It was the longest minute of his life. Every time the doors opened on another level, he had felt his breath back up in his throat, but he made it.

As he stepped into the hallway, he mentally patted himself on the back for not weeping or shaking.

Briefly, he glanced at Delta's door and wondered what she was doing, if she was home or out saving lives. When the door did nothing but remain closed, he unlocked his own.

Just as he closed the door behind him, his phone rang.

"Sullivan." His voice was brisk, his tone arrogant.

"*Sullivan*," came his brother's mocking voice, "You know you do have caller ID, and I know whom I'm calling, so it's not necessary to throw that prosecutor tone at me." Caleb laughed.

"Caleb," Neal said. It was always good to hear from his brother. "Kill anyone today?"

A brisk laugh came over the phone. "No, actually I'm collecting evidence."

His eldest brother was the famous crime writer Caleb Sullivan, who had written not one but two New York Times bestsellers.

"That sounds interesting," Neal said, confused. It still baffled him how his brother enjoyed writing about the horrors most people wanted to forget.

"Don't worry, I won't ask you for any advice on this one."

"Good. How's Sarah? Is she running around making beds or painting?"

"She doesn't make beds," Caleb grunted. "She supervises the whole damn Oak Cottages, and the paint fumes are bad for the baby."

Neal could hear his brother smile. "Baby? What baby? Your baby?"

"Yup," came the gloating voice over the phone.

"You sure as hell didn't waste any time. The wedding was

barely two months ago!"

"Seven weeks, to be exact, but who's counting?" Caleb laughed.

"Is she grumpy and tired? I remember Dad said Mom was like a bear with a sore tooth every time she got pregnant."

"Well, besides the banana and mustard sandwiches, everything's fine. How are things on your end?"

"Great, well actually, they are now. Let's just say I won't be getting into an elevator without fear for some time."

"Why? Did something happen?" Caleb asked, concerned.

"I got stuck in the elevator at work last night."

"Let me guess: you were the last person in the building and ended up waiting hours before someone came to the rescue? Oh, and while you were in there you probably wrote about a dozen briefs."

Neal laughed awkwardly. He wasn't about to tell his brother that he was scared. "Actually, she rescued me shortly after I got stuck."

"She?" Caleb asked with genuine interest.

"Yes, a female firefighter."

"What? That's impressive. You at least get her number?"

Caleb was big believer in happy ever afters; since he met his wife Sarah, he had been pushing his happiness on everyone.

"No, actually, I met her this morning in the hallway outside my apartment. She lives across from me."

"No way! What are the chances? So are you finally going to try dating again?"

"I don't know. Last night there was something I could've almost called attraction, but this morning when I recognized her, she looked like a deer caught in the headlights. Strange…" Neal trailed off, confused again by Sarah's reaction.

"What do you mean? She wasn't happy to see you, or you basically hounded her to thank her for rescuing you?"

"No, at first she was surprised that we live across from each other, but then she…I don't know Caleb… it was like she was scared. Like she had a fright or flight moment or something. She all but ran into her apartment, locking the door behind her."

"Isn't it fight or flight?"

"That's just it, she had a fright and then she fled into her apartment."

"It sounds strange, Neal. If I were you, I'd rather keep my distance."

"That's what I thought as well, but I don't know, Caleb, there is just something about her that I'd like to get to know better."

Caleb laughed. "Well, I'll be... This must be the first time in about a decade you spent a whole phone call talking about a girl."

"I've talked about women before; besides, I spoke more about my near-death experience," Neal defended himself.

"Oh really, like when? And if you didn't even write a brief or suffer an injury, I barely call it near-death."

"Like..." Neal trailed off, failing to remember one phone call when he had spoken about a girl.

"Exactly. Listen, Neal, if you're interested, find out what that something is. All I'm saying is she sounds complicated and might even come with baggage. Just be careful."

As Neal ended the call, he thought back to Caleb's words. *Just be careful.*

The oddity of it was that Neal always followed the rules, played things safe. For once in his life, he was willing to take a chance and follow his instincts and live on the wild side. *I mean,* he thought, *I finally had the pizza with olives and Parmesan.*

Chapter 4

DELTA SAT DOWN with her bowl of scrambled eggs and switched on the television. Nothing comforted her more than cheesy eggs when she was feeling down or had a hard day. It was her ultimate comfort food. Right now, she needed nothing more.

She channel-hopped until she found a rerun of a nineties sitcom. After she had settled on the couch, her mind drifted back to Neal Sullivan.

Neal Sullivan. Even his name sent thrills rushing through her.

When she was faced with him that morning, she had been momentarily stunned before she had been happily surprised to find out he was her neighbor. He was freshly showered; drops of water still clung to the ends of his hair, and the scent of his sandalwood aftershave drifted to her, making her heart beat a little faster.

MAN FAST! MAN FAST! MAN FAST!

She kept chanting the words in her mind, trying to push the attraction and all thoughts of Neal away.

That would make for interesting comings and goings, she couldn't help but think as she stared at the television, not paying any attention to what was on-screen.

After the elevator incident, she had thought it was different with him, that the panic and fear that clutched at her throat when a man came near didn't apply to him.

And yet when he had leaned closer, the fear had almost paralyzed her. Maybe she should see a therapist after all. The strangest part was that it never affected her at work; her mind told her it was because she was always in control at work.

Craig had taken all her control and abused it.

She had been a capable and strong-minded girl when she met Craig. Delta had left him a beaten and broken woman, no longer gullible to his wiles and charm. She set the bowl down after polishing off the eggs. But she refused to believe that Craig had broken her. He had hurt her, bruised her ego, and broken her trust in men, but he didn't break her. She smiled at the thought, knowing she walked out on him, and she fell asleep dreaming of her neighbor with the deep blue eyes.

Delta locked her apartment door behind her. After forty-eight hours of almost no rest, she was glad to be heading to the firehouse. She had woken from horrible nightmares and checked all the locks on the front door countless times. *It will get better,* she promised herself as she locked her apartment. It was a new beginning; she just needed to give her mind time to catch up.

As she stepped into the elevator, she saw Neal come out of his apartment.

"Hold it," he shouted as he ran towards the open doors.

Delta placed her hand between the sliding doors and kept it there until Neal was standing next to her.

"Thank you, I'm running late," Neal said as he pressed the button for the ground floor, a frown creasing his forehead.

"No problem, glad to know you're not perpetually scarred from using elevators after the other night," Delta teased. She found herself feeling comfortable with Neal, as long as he wasn't too close.

Neal laughed. "I'll have you know there are nine floors between the ground and my office. I spent one day climbing stairs and decided I'll need to get over my fear or find another job."

Delta smiled at him as his woodsy aftershave drifted over her.

Woodsy, definitely not sandalwood, she thought as her eyes met his.

A smile shined in them before he spoke. "I wanted to send you flowers."

"Excuse me?" Delta asked, surprised and still wondering about his scent.

"For saving me," Neal explained.

"That really isn't necessary. Besides, if it were one of my crew, I bet you wouldn't have the urge to send them flowers."

Neal thought for a moment about sending flowers to a hairy guy with arms the size of tree stumps. "Nope, can't say I would."

"Exactly." Delta smiled at him. "Besides, I get enough flack for being a girl as it is, throw in some flowers with the feminist issue, and they'll give me even more grief."

"I can imagine." Neal watched her, fascinated. "I'll make you a deal: I won't send you flowers if you have dinner with me."

"I can't." Delta shrugged. "I'm on for the next twenty-four."

"That means you'll be off Friday morning?"

Delta nodded. "That's right, and then I'm going to sleep."

"Great, you'll sleep all day and be at my place at seven." Neal smiled at her as the elevator doors opened, as if the matter was settled.

Delta stepped out in front of him, confused by the fact that even though she was going to say no, she had actually for a moment considered it. "I didn't say yes, Mr. Sullivan," she threw carelessly over her shoulder.

Neal smiled at her. "You didn't say no, either; invitation's open. I'll cook, and you can sit back, relax, and judge my culinary prowess."

Delta couldn't help but laugh. Something about this man interested her, and she didn't feel that threatening clutch at her throat when he looked into her eyes. He looked stern and every bit the businessman he was...but he didn't look cruel.

She had come to enjoy seeing the frown disappear and a light of humor shine in his eyes. If she felt like it, maybe she would mosey on over Friday night, and try to chase away his frown again.

It was a busy shift for Delta. They had call after call, giving her little to no time to ponder over the dinner invitation from Neal. She had always enjoyed being a firefighter, except for shifts like the one that had just come to an end.

Shifts when they lost someone.

When they had tried everything, even risking their own lives in order to save someone they didn't know. Walking out of that building and facing the man crying on the sidewalk was heart-wrenching.

The chief had pulled them back when he noticed the smoke change, realizing the building was about to go.

Delta had pushed forward, but one of her crew had pulled her back, calling her stupid for wanting to go back. Delta hated it when they had to leave someone behind. Her heart ached for the man that had just lost his wife.

She had pulled through the rest of the shift grateful every time they were called, so she wouldn't have the time to wallow in what ifs. What if they had gotten there sooner? What if they had gotten the wife out first?

When she stumbled into her apartment Friday morning, she still wasn't sure if she wanted to go that evening.

Neal looked like a decent guy but so did Craig, at first. What if he also turned out to be a Craig?

A man that enjoyed hurting woman to feel powerful. Her skin sprung goosebumps at the thought of how quickly a man could change. Yet she had seen something in his eyes, a kindness or pain that pulled her in.

She was on a man-fast; she didn't need or have to go to dinner. But she had to admit she was curious about the first man she'd been attracted to in six months. A man that looked serious and yet, when he smiled, there was a child-like glint in his eyes. She wanted to learn more about him and about what had put that serious look in his eye.

Delta took a quick shower, ruthlessly washing the smoke and soot from her face and hair before crashing into her bed.

Too tired to ponder on Neal's dinner invitation any longer, she decided to sleep on it and see how she felt when she woke up that evening.

Delta woke up with a start to a taxi honking, seemingly right outside her window.

She reached for her phone and opened her eyes just enough to see the time. For a moment, she didn't believe the time on the phone; she glanced out the window. Judging by the low light, her phone was right.

It was already twenty past seven.

Shit!

She was already late, and she still wanted to put on a little makeup before she went over to Neal's. She sat up in bed with her heart jumping a mile a minute, wondering when she had decided to actually go.

It was already too late; she might as well stay at home and watch an old movie.

Even as she decided to stay home, she found herself standing up and marching into the bathroom; if she was going to Neal's, she needed to wake up first.

She flicked on the shower and quickly undressed. As she stepped into the shower, she realized she was slightly nervous about going over, even if it was only for dinner.

Strangely, it wasn't the same kind of nerves she had experienced since she left Craig. The fear kind that left you weak and trembling in anticipation of being hurt.

It was the jittery kind that came with excitement.

Delta smiled at herself as she dressed; just maybe, she was healing faster than anticipated.

Chapter 5

ACROSS THE HALL from Delta's apartment, Neal was just sliding the chicken pie into the oven.

What if she doesn't come? he thought to himself. He would be having leftover chicken pie the rest of the weekend.

He grabbed a bottled of chilled white wine from the fridge and poured himself a glass. It was already past seven, and disappointment was seeping through the cracks. He had been confident she would come. That she would be as curious about him as he was about her.

It seemed she was going to prove him wrong. He thought back again to the fear in her eyes when he had stepped closer. Neal had seen enough abused clients to know when a woman had been abused.

He wondered if she had ever gone to the police. Was she

getting counseling? He took another sip of wine and decided if she wasn't coming; it wasn't worth him spending the whole night thinking about her. He pulled out his latest case file and started working.

Another glass of wine and long while later, there was a brief knock on the door. Neal checked the time; it was already past eight. If it was Delta, he should just tell her to go home.

But he knew he wouldn't. He was sure if it was her, she would have a good excuse for being late.

He sauntered over to the door, forcing himself to take his time; he didn't want to seem too eager

"Delta?" He asked with a question in his eyes as he opened the door. "I didn't think you were coming."

It was the first time Neal saw her as a woman and not the firefighter that saved him. She was wearing dark blue skinny jeans and a soft pale green cashmere top. Her eyes were watching him hesitantly.

She had put some of that female stuff on her face to make her eyes look bigger. He took her in; her skin was flawless, and her hands were holding onto each other so tightly that her knuckles were white. "I overslept." Even though her voice was soft, it held no apology.

Neal looked at her, confused for a minute before it dawned on him. She worked until seven this morning; she had been sleeping the whole day.

Her soft blonde curls were framing her face, and she was biting her bottom lip. Neal couldn't help but wonder if it was as soft as it looked. The scent of her vanilla perfume drifted to him.

"Of course, no problem. I didn't think you were going to come."

Delta stepped inside and was carefully looking around when her stomach growled.

"Hungry?" he asked with a wink.

Delta laughed. "I haven't eaten since this morning."

"Well, the pie is almost ready. Would you like to start with a glass of wine?"

Following him into the kitchen, Delta sat down at the kitchen island on a stool. She noticed all the paperwork spread out, and before she could ask, Neal gathered the papers and placed them efficiently in his briefcase.

"Sorry, since I thought you weren't coming, I started on some work."

"Here you go," Neal said as he placed the glass of wine in front of her. He picked up his own and toasted her.

"To the damsel that helped me when I was distressed."

"Cheers." She merely smiled before standing up and walking towards the oven to take a peek at the chicken pie. "It smells wonderful."

"Family recipe," Neal said behind her. She suddenly stood up straight and moved back to her seat at the counter.

Neal couldn't help but notice she was uncomfortable and thought back to his hunch of abuse. If it were the case, that wouldn't be a conversation he would approach tonight. It would take a lot more than a glass of wine and a warm dinner for her to tell him about that.

Changing tactics, he asked her about something he hoped would help her relax a little. "So how does a woman decide to become a firefighter?"

Delta laughed. "If I had a penny for every time a man asked me that." She sipped on her wine watching him over the rim of the glass. "How does a man decide to become a nurse? That has always been a female occupation, and yet every year more men become nurses."

"Touché."

"But to answer your question is easy. My father was a firefighter, and I always went with him to the firehouse. I was an only child, so I was little spoiled, but not in the materialistic sense. My parents spent time with me and made me enjoy spending time with them."

"Do they live close?" Neal asked, wondering what her father would be like and if he knew about the abuse. If Delta had been his daughter, the man who had put that look in her eye wouldn't be walking the earth anymore.

"No, my father went into a burning school ten years ago and saved fourteen children, but he never came out when he went in for the fifteenth." She took a big gulp of wine, the pain and loss still evident in her voice and her eyes. "And my mother died of cancer three years ago."

Neal gently placed his hand over hers. "That must've been really hard, I'm sorry."

Delta smiled sadly. "It was." Neal felt her hand tense beneath his for a moment before she relaxed and continued. "Anyway, so I spent summers in the firehouse; my dad's crew taught me how to cook and everything about fires. It was a natural step from there for me. I wanted to save people the way they did every day."

"It isn't a natural step for many people to put their lives at stake every day for others." Neal looked deep into her eyes and softly stroked her hand with his thumb.

"No, it isn't, is it?" Delta asked thoughtfully

"Do you enjoy it?" Neal asked, enjoying the feel of her skin beneath his touch and the cadence of her voice as she spoke.

"Yes actually, I do. I know it sounds a bit cliché, but I've always been an adrenaline junkie. I love the rush, the adrenaline pumping through your veins just after you've doused a fire or saved a life."

"The training must be quite intense."

"It is; you'd think they'd lower the standards for women, but they don't. And its better that way; otherwise, it would give the male firefighters even more reason to give me grief."

"Do you train every day?" Neal asked, losing himself in the dark green color of her eyes.

"Not every day, but I work out at least three times a week, and we do quite a few drills at the firehouse when we're not on call."

Neal cocked his brow. "Wow, then you're probably really fit? Fitter than I am, certainly."

Delta laughed, a carefree sound flowing through the room. "Let's just say I wouldn't have a problem climbing eight flights of stairs multiple times a day."

Neal smiled, even more intrigued. Not only was she interesting but she was witty as well. "I must say, you're not what I expected."

Neal looked into her emerald green eyes, surprised that for the first time in years he was intrigued by a woman enough to want to spend more time with her.

"What did you expect?" Delta asked, tilting her chin curiously.

"Let's just say I'd take the fifth on that." Neal took another sip of wine with his free hand as Delta's stiffened beneath his. She briskly pulled it away.

"Are you a lawyer?" Delta's voice was serious, the witty tone gone. "We saved you from the elevator in the courthouse; of course you must be a lawyer. How didn't I see that?" she said almost to herself.

"Yes, I am. Is that a problem?"

She twirled the wine glass in her hand before answering sarcastically, "Since I'm just your neighbor, no, it isn't."

Neal picked up her irritation immediately. "Do you have a

problem with lawyers in general, or is it just me?"

"Let's just say I've seen what a high-powered job can to do a man; I'm not interested in a rerun."

Neal started putting the pieces together; the man who hurt her must've been a lawyer. "I'm a prosecutor for the State of Delaware. I'm one of the good guys." Neal saw her watching him doubtfully. "I put the bad guys behind bars, Delta."

Delta smiled sadly. "That's what they all say."

Neal felt his temper start to rise. She wouldn't allow him to judge her career choice, but she felt entitled to judge his? "Did a lawyer hurt you or make a case against you?"

"No." Her voice was soft and unconvincing. The answer was obviously a lie.

Knowing he wasn't going to get to the bottom of the issue after one glass of wine, Neal put it aside. "Well, let's put my job aside and enjoy dinner. Besides, you're hungry." He cocked his brow in question.

Delta watched him cautiously just as her stomach growled again. "All right, I can't argue with that."

"That must've been the best chicken and mushroom pie I have ever had. Neal, I must say, if you cook like this every night, I might make a habit of arriving for dinner," Delta said as she pushed her plate aside.

During dinner, they had talked about the weather, Wilmington in general, and the public transport system. The tension that had gripped her ever since Neal had mentioned he was a lawyer had dissipated enough for her to joke with him again, but Neal knew it was still lurking in the back of her mind. "I wouldn't mind, you're welcome any time."

"Careful what you say, my friend: my metabolism is much faster than yours, and I can guarantee you one day I'll shock you with my appetite."

Neal laughed; she wasn't lying. She had two pieces of chicken pie and had eaten with an appetite he hadn't seen in many women.

Most women picked at their plates, or they would ask for a lighter option. For a moment, he wondered if he had subconsciously made the pie to see what her reaction would be. Obviously, she had enjoyed it. "It's good to finally meet a woman who isn't afraid to eat."

Delta laughed, her eyes lighting up at the backhanded

compliment.

"Coffee, or would you prefer tea?" Neal said as he carried their dishes to the sink.

"Let's live on the wild side and have some coffee." Delta carried their wine glasses to the kitchen and sat down on the barstool. "I overslept anyhow, so coffee or no coffee, I'll be up most of the night."

"It probably takes getting used to, being awake for twenty-four hours at a time?" Neal asked as he started the coffee machine.

The scent of freshly ground beans permeated the air as Carly Simon's voice carried through from the living room.

"It was in the beginning, but we're not awake the whole shift. We sleep in shifts between calls."

They sat down in the living room with their coffee, listening to old music and discussing their favorite bands late into the night.

Neal was relieved to see Delta had relaxed enough to kick off her shoes and fold her feet underneath her. She closed her eyes as Van Morrison started singing, lightly swaying to the music.

Lost in thought, Neal brushed a stray strand of her hair from her face. He felt her stiffen slightly at the touch. Neal watched her watching him. She didn't move when he touched her, although she didn't encourage it either. He leaned a little closer, watching her. She still didn't move.

He could feel the attraction simmer between them and could swear he saw it in her eyes, but beneath it he still saw the fear. He gently leaned in and softly pressed his lips against hers. Her lips were soft and giving under his; he wanted more but didn't want to scare her.

He slowly leaned back and watched her eyes flutter open.

"This isn't a good idea." As she spoke the words, Neal noticed fear had clouded her eyes again. She sat up and hastily slipped on her shoes.

"It certainly wasn't a bad idea." Neal tried to defend himself.

She looked at him with those big green eyes, once again the deer in the headlights. Without another word, she grabbed her keys and ran out.

Neal heard the door slam behind her and berated himself. He should've taken it slower, but something about Delta made him want more. She intrigued and fascinated him at the same time. Before anything could happen between them again Neal needed to find out what had put that look in her eye.

Chapter 6

DELTA SLAMMED THE door behind her and triple-locked it for the night. What just happened? Neal was nothing like Craig, so why did fear clutch her throat even as her heart beat erratically from his kiss?

Neal had done everything to make her feel welcome. She certainly hadn't enjoyed a home-cooked meal like that in a long time, and yet a few times, she had been scared. Throughout the evening, she had focused on the feeling she had in-between being scared: attraction.

It felt foreign to her and warred with the reminders her subconscious kept throwing her way about how she had crawled out of her apartment in Chicago. If it weren't for Neal's proximity and her curiosity over her attraction for him, Delta never would've gone. In fact, she should've left when he said the word lawyer.

Craig had been a lawyer, an important man with a lot of stress. Delta had convinced herself it must've been the stress that had turned him into a ruthless monster with steel fists. Maybe while they attended law school potential lawyers were taught to take their stress out on people close to them and not their clients, but deep down, she knew the truth.

Nothing had changed him; he had just kept that part hidden very well. What if Neal was hiding a part of himself as well? No one invited you to dinner and served the main course with a side of "Hey, I'm a beater."

She felt her breathing calm down to an acceptable rate and moved from where she was still standing with her back against the door to the couch. After wrapping herself in the blanket she had left there earlier, she went over the evening again.

Either his apartment had been cleaned for her benefit or Neal was a very tidy person; for some reason, Delta leaned more towards the last. The furnishings were minimalistic but high quality and had no signs of wear. Either everything was brand new or Neal didn't spend a lot of time at home; again Delta leaned towards the last.

He had been jovial and had even once or twice forgotten about his constant frown and smiled at her. Those were the times Delta felt attraction, hot and exciting, pulsing in her veins.

When he had mentioned being a lawyer, Delta had felt the fear tingle up her spine; she had even scanned for the nearest exit...and then he smiled.

Something fuzzy had curled in her belly and heated her blood. She had the same feeling buzz through her system seconds before he kissed her, until his hand reached for her. Attraction had vanished like mist in the sun, and it was replaced with a heart-clutching fear. Delta had been certain she was going to have a panic attack right there in front of Neal, so instead did the only thing she was good at these days...running.

Now safely cocooned in her blanket behind locked doors, she allowed herself to think of Neal's smile. He certainly used it sparingly, but when he did, he was the most attractive man Delta had ever met.

"Good morning, everyone," Shae said, smiling kindly. "I want you all to know this is a safe environment where you won't be judged, but you will be heard."

Delta sat back against the cold steel of the folding chair in the local library and felt Shae's calmness wash over her.

Joining Shae's group – Fighting Back – was the best thing Delta had done when she had arrived in Wilmington. Not too long ago, it was Delta that sat hunched on her chair with bruises on her face and Shae's hand on her arm.

"Welcome, Rose," Shae said to the newcomer beside her and turned to group. Everyone knew her part and how much it meant the first time.

"Welcome, Rose," their voices chorused.

Shae sat back and smiled at the group of abused women before asking gently, "Who'd like to share?"

Next to her, Delta noticed through her peripheral vision, sat Nadine. Ever since her first meeting, Delta had been fearful of Nadine. She looked tough, and from the stories she had told in the group, she no doubt was. Nadine wore leather tights that hugged her thighs so tightly that the seams were stretched, with a leather jacket and big chunky silver rings dangling from her ears. Even as Delta listened to a woman sharing her story, she couldn't help but think she didn't want to get on Nadine's bad side.

For the forty-five minutes, women took turns sharing their stories and how far they were on their road to recovery, not only physically but emotionally as well. As always, Delta sat and listened; that was enough for her. To know she wasn't the only person who didn't see it coming and to know that she would be able to work past the fear like some of the woman in the group had.

"I'd like you all to think about something for next time. You don't have to answer me now, or even share at our next meeting, but I'd like you to give this a thought. When do you know you are ready to trust a man again?"

At the hushed whispers and eyes widening around the room, Shae laughed kindly. "Like I said, just mull it over. Until next week everyone."

All the ladies stood and joined hands before they said their mantra.

"With broken wings

We stand together

Like birds of a feather.

We now know we do not lack,

And we can FIGHT BACK!"

They bid each other goodbye; some stayed to chat, while others rushed out. As Delta bent to pick up her purse, she heard

Nadine's gravelly voice above her.

"She got it wrong, man, at least for me. It ain't 'bout learning to trust again, it's about learning which man you can trust."

Delta stood up and hooked her purse over her shoulder. "I think you're right, at least to me. I'm having that problem."

Nadine smiled, a broad friendly smile showing perfect white teeth against her coffee-colored skin. "Come on, honey, I think you need to tell Nadine over a cup of coffee."

Delta's first instinct was to refuse, but she actually needed to talk about it. So she held out her hand. "Delta Eckhart."

Nadine laughed. "Nice to meet you, Delta Eckhart, I didn't know you could talk. Heavens knows you haven't shared anything since you joined FIGHT BACK. I'm Nadine L'amour."

Delta smiled. "Pleased to meet you, Nadine. You've got a beautiful surname."

"Let's just say I'm from Alabama and that even though my family came from slaves, my grandmother caught a Frenchman's interest."

Laughing together, they moved to where the coffee station had been set up for the meeting. Once they each had a cup, Nadine with three sugars no cream, and Delta without any sugar and a generous dollop of cream, they sat down.

It was Nadine who spoke first. "Maybe that's my trouble; I like my men like I like my coffee, sweet with a dark soul."

Delta nearly spat out her coffee.

"Don't you worry, honey. I've been around the block too many times not to know where I go wrong. So what went wrong with you?"

Delta had never told anyone about Chicago or Craig and for the first time since getting off that midnight bus, she wanted to share her story. "I met a man - kind, smart, and charming - and fell head over heels in love. For two years, I fell a little deeper every day, until he hit me the first time."

"Asshole!" Nadine said in a huff. "You leave?"

"No. The second time I tried reporting it, but let's just say as an influential lawyer in Chicago, he pulled a few strings." Delta sipped on her bitter coffee and looked straight into Nadine's dark brown eyes. "The third time, though, I waited till he passed out and took the first bus heading east."

"Well at least you took the bus; it took some of these girls years before they gathered the courage to leave. Hell, it took me waking up in hospital to realize I had to leave the last guy."

"I think subconsciously I knew if I didn't leave that night, I wouldn't leave at all."

"See, that right there I don't have," Nadine said pointing to Delta's face. "I think my subconscious went on holiday about the time I started dating."

"Well, my subconscious is all over the radar at the moment, with my neighbor."

"Do tell…" Nadine said, leaning closer.

"I met him on duty; he was stuck in an elevator." At Nadine's frown, Delta smiled. "I'm a firefighter. So anyway, I bump into him the next day in my building; he's my neighbor."

"So what's the problem?"

"I think I'm attracted to him, but how do I know he's not just another Craig that's going to beat me in a year or two?"

Nadine thought for a long moment. "I take it you took Shae's advice when you started coming here about the man-fast?"

"Yes." Delta laughed. "As stupid as it sounds, I think it's a great idea."

"Well in my experience, if you're attracted to someone, your man-fast has expired."

"I'm not sure I'm ready to be attracted."

"Then just be friends. Seems to me if he's your neighbor you're going to be seeing more of him, so you might as well be friendly. Learn to trust one guy as a friend before you try doing it again in a relationship."

Delta chewed her lower lip. "Nadine, I think that's a great idea. Maybe if I spend time with him, as a friend, I'll get over my fear of men as well."

"See, we needed to have coffee."

"We did, although I will admit I was afraid of you."

"Me? Why on earth would you be afraid of me? You're a firefighter!"

Delta laughed. "I might be a firefighter, but you look strong, not physically necessarily, but emotionally. Like you're a tough person. I remember you saying in group that after you recovered in the hospital, you went and beat that guy right back. I wish I could be tougher."

"It's was different for me. It wasn't my first time at the rodeo, and I knew he'd be coming home drunk the night I pounced him." Smiling, Nadine punched Delta's arm lightly. "We'll just have to toughen you up some."

That evening, Delta was making cheesy eggs, still thinking about Nadine's advice. If she were to become friends with Neal, it would assuage her fear and maybe she could learn to trust him. Once that happened, she could decide whether or not to act on their attraction. She had just spooned the food onto her plate when there was a brief knock on her door.

"Coming," she called out as she touched the hot pan to her wrist. "Shit!" She tossed the pan into the sink with a clatter before grabbing an ice cube and rubbing it on her wrist as she moved to the door.

She opened it to find Neal standing there in a suit with a candy bouquet looking as foolish as she was sure he felt.

Delta couldn't stop the laugh that bubbled up. "Neal?"

"I didn't know whether to apologize for whatever happened last night or to say thank you for the elevator, so this will say both."

Delta took the candy bouquet from him; it was the weirdest and most whimsical gift she had ever received. "I'll take it as a thank you; you don't need to apologize for last night. That's on me."

"Mind if I come inside?" Neal asked.

Delta's smile momentarily slipped at the thought of being alone with a man in her apartment before she shook it off. "Sure, come in."

Neal followed her inside and stood just inside the door, taking in her apartment. "This is nice, suits you."

"Thanks, I like it anyway. Still needs some wall hangings, though."

Neal nodded; he clearly had something on his mind. "About last night, what exactly happened? The one moment I thought we had a moment and the next you rushed out the door like your pants were on fire."

Delta swallowed the giggle; if only he knew for a few seconds there she had been on fire for him. "It wasn't you, Neal. Honestly, it was me. I'm not looking for a...." Delta chewed on her bottom lip, looking for the right word, "complication."

Neal's smile faded, and his frown reappeared. "Last night didn't feel all that complicated to me."

Delta smiled and sensed Neal moving closer. Her heart galloped at thought of kissing him again. She knew she had to stop him, but she couldn't. She angled her head, waiting for his lips to rest against her.

His lips were smooth and warm and barely grazed hers. The hot contrast of his lips with the ice on her skin sent her into sensory overdrive. She felt that jolt of attraction kick-starting her hormones that had been slumbering for so long. The kiss started to turn heavier, and Delta felt Neal's hand against the nape of her neck. In a fraction of a second, fear clasped her throat and turned her knees to statues. She drew back, panting, "Please, leave."

"Delta?" Neal asked, confused about her reaction.

"Just..." Delta's breath was coming too fast. She knew she was going to pass out if she didn't calm down. "Leave!"

Neal shook his head, confused, before turning around and leaving her apartment, slamming the door behind him.

As soon as he was gone, Delta managed to calm her breathing. She sat down to a cold plate of cheesy eggs, knowing she was wrong to lead Neal on. Delta didn't want to give him the wrong impression, but when those sapphire-blue eyes zoned in on hers, she was helpless to the attraction she felt for him. She ate her cheesy eggs staring at the candy bouquet and wondering what type of man would think of buying a candy bouquet for a woman.

Chapter 7

EVER SINCE HIS first high school crush, Neal had never lost sleep over a girl. Until now. He had a hunch about why Delta nearly had a panic attack every time he touched her, but at the same time, he could see she felt the same way as him.

For the past few days, he had only seen her when she left her apartment or came home from a shift looking beat. Even though she was friendly and greeted him, she couldn't get away from him fast enough. That was why, when he got home late one evening, he was surprised to find a note slipped under his door.

Dinner tomorrow night at 7, my place.

Delta

Neal cursed and crumpled the little note in his fist before tossing it in the bin. This was stupid; he was too old for cat and mouse games, especially with a woman who ran hot the one minute and turned to ice the next.

He tugged off his tie and poured himself a glass of red wine. The dark red liquid slipped down his throat like velvet. With a sigh, he put down the glass and retrieved the note from the trash.

He carefully unfolded it and read it again. There was no hint of what he could expect from the dinner: an apology, a request to leave her alone, nothing. Neal hated the fact that that intrigued him even more.

He opened his current case file and was absorbed in what he needed to do tomorrow in court. There was no use spending time to mull over Delta's invite because Neal already knew he was going, even if it was just out of curiosity.

The following evening, Neal stood outside Delta's door in a good mood with a bottle of wine in his hand. He had a good day in court, and he knew the jury was empathetic with his client. If the case proceeded like it did today, justice would be served.

He knocked twice and heard Delta's voice call from inside, "It's open!"

Neal slowly opened the door and stepped inside, not knowing

what to expect. The frightful deer or the women with a smile like sunshine.

"You came," Delta said wiping her hands on a dishrag as Neal stood beside the small kitchen island.

Neal took her in; there were no shadows in her eyes tonight. He smiled, "Well, you invited me."

"I did, and I'm so glad you came. I wanted to apologize..." She trailed off and focused on cutting vegetables before taking a deep breath and putting down the knife. Her forest-green eyes met his. "I'm sorry, I know you must think I'm crazy since I either run or kick you out every time I see you."

"Well, I can't say I enjoy the brisk endings of our evenings together as much as I enjoy the conversation that precedes them."

Delta laughed. "Maybe one day I'll explain."

Neal watched a shadow briefly pass over her face before she smiled at him brightly again. "I hope you like stir-fry?"

"As long as there's some meat in there somewhere, I'm fine with stir-fry."

Delta took out wineglasses and gave them to Neal, who had already opened the bottle of wine he brought. "Sorry, no meat in the stir-fry." Delta turned around and took a plate out of the fridge with two large steaks on it. "I prefer my meat on the side."

Neal laughed at the size of the steaks. Judging by her appetite the night she came to him for dinner, he was sure she would finish every bite of it. "It's a good thing I brought red wine then."

"Yes, it is," Delta said as she focused on cutting the peppers and the mushrooms.

Neal watched as Delta cooked. Every move was controlled and had purpose. It seemed to him she didn't waste a single ounce of energy. He also noticed she kept the kitchen counter firmly between them the whole time.

When the stir-fry was done, Neal refilled their glasses and watched Delta pull an iron skillet out of a cupboard and toss some olive oil in.

She turned to him with an easy smile, her honey-blonde curls bouncing on her shoulders. She wore frayed jeans with a simple white long-sleeved T-shirt, no makeup adorned her face, and her lips were a natural light pink. The punch of attraction hit him strong in the gut, and he couldn't help but wonder why. Delta wasn't what you would call beautiful; she had a sharp chin and angled cheekbones, but her nose was cute. Her eyes were big enough to get lost in, but her forehead was slightly small; overall, her face was more intriguing than pretty. And every time Neal looked hard and long enough, like now, he found her even more intriguing.

"How do you like your steak?" Delta asked, frowning at Neal's obvious assessment.

"Raw to medium," Neal answered, still surveying her face.

"Great! Me too."

Delta slapped a steak in the cast iron pan. It instantly sizzled, and the air filled with the aromatic fragrance of steak and spices.

"You're not beautiful," Neal said and wanted to smack himself when he realized he had said it aloud.

Delta laughed and turned to him, "Why Neal, you're not one for compliments, are you?"

Neal shrugged. "You don't look to me like the type of woman that needs them, much less the type that expects them."

Delta thought for a moment and gave him a high wattage smile. "I've never thought of it like that, but you're right. I don't, and I'm not beautiful."

"But you are interesting, and I have a feeling that you're strong, stronger than most women."

"Well since I'm a firefighter, I can attest to that," she said, flipping over the steak to sizzle on the other side.

"I'm not talking about physical strength, Delta; I'm talking about the kind that earns respect."

"Wow, this turned really deep really fast." She gripped the steak with a fork and set it on a plate in front of Neal before slapping her own in the pan.

Neal sipped and watched her over the glass. *Definitely not the kind that appreciated compliments either.* "The steak looks good." He stood up and moved around the kitchen island to dish up the stir-fry. He had barely entered the kitchen when Delta turned around with an uncomfortable smile.

"No, you go sit down. I'll dish up the stir-fry for you." Neal moved back to his seat and watched as she gave him a healthy serving of stir-fry. So she was intentionally keeping the kitchen island between them.

"Thank you," Neal said when Delta sat down next to him with her plate.

"It's a pleasure, dig in." Neal laughed when she did just that. There was something to say about a woman that had a healthy appetite; Neal had never thought about it but somehow found it very appealing.

Neal followed her lead. There was nothing fancy about the meal, but it was delicious in its simplicity. As she ate, Delta barely spoke, focusing on the meal in front of her. By the time both their plates were cleared, Delta moved back to her spot behind the kitchen island and put their plates in the sink.

"Would you like some coffee?" The tenseness from sitting next to him visibly diminished as she put more space between them.

"Sure, cream no sugar."

Delta laughed. "Me too."

She made the coffee and invited Neal to join her on the small balcony with their coffee.

The evening still had a hint of chill, but it was refreshing.

"So you mentioned you're a lawyer last time?" Delta asked, gripping her coffee mug with white knuckles.

"Yes, I am. I've always wanted to be one, to fight for justice; however clichéd that might sound, it's true."

"You ever come up against the fancy private lawyers?" Delta asked with a nervous voice.

"Every day, and most days I beat them." Neal wasn't bragging, but he had a feeling Delta needed to know that.

She visibly relaxed. "That's good."

"Delta, I don't mean to pry, but what have you got against lawyers?" Neal asked, putting his hand over hers.

Delta sighed. "Neal, I'd like to be friends, but then you need to stop probing."

Neal cocked his head. "I thought we were having a conversation. Now I do know you have something against lawyers, and you're just not willing to tell me. Which means I won't stop wondering until you tell me?"

Delta stuck out her chin. "Good luck with that. I'd rather not talk about it."

"Fine," Neal said, feeling his temper rise. "Then let's talk about this: why do you want to be my friend?"

Delta laughed. "Because you seem like a nice honest person."

"Wrong answer, Delta," Neal said. Delta looked at him with that fearful expression and stood up.

"Thank you for coming, it was a nice evening." Her voice held a dismissive tone, and it irked Neal even more than her answer.

He followed her into the kitchen and crowded her in, ignoring the fear in her eyes. "You know there's something here, already more than friendship. I felt it that first night and every other time we spend time together. Why are you denying it?"

Delta's gaze didn't move from his. "Like I said, I'd like us to be friends."

Neal leaned in and watched her eyes lower as she waited for his kiss. He drew on all his control not to kiss her, instead simply whispering against her lips, "You can keep telling yourself that, but you know this is more than that."

Delta gasped, and her eyes flew open to meet his.

Neal grinned easily as he stepped back. "But don't worry, Delta. I won't kiss you again. I'm a patient man, one that knows delayed gratification is better than instant, and with you, I have a feeling it's going to be worth the wait."

Delta's eyes widened at his words, but before she could say something, Neal continued, "So I'll be your friend, Delta, and I won't touch you until you ask me to because I know sooner or later you're going to ask me."

Neal grabbed his keys on the kitchen island and glanced at Delta a final time before leaving, hoping to hell he was right.

Chapter 8

"HEY DELTA, YOU coming or going?" Delta jumped at the mention of her name but quickly relaxed when she realized it was Neal locking his own door across the hall.

She turned around and felt the easy smile spread across her face. His hair was still slightly damp, his jaw shaved cleaned. He wore a charcoal suit with a light blue shirt and a navy tie. She hoped to hell the opposing counsel wasn't a woman because if it was, Delta knew she would be as distracted as Delta was right now.

"Hi Neal, actually, I'm heading out. You're leaving early for work; it's barely six am." Delta tossed her keys in the small leather satchel she used as a handbag and walked with Neal to the elevator.

"Yeah, I'm in court most of the day, so I quickly want to catch up with some things before the day begins."

"It's a tough life," Delta teased.

Neal let his gaze travel over her jeans and WFD T-shirt before meeting her gaze. "Back at you. You working twenty-four?"

Delta shook her head. "No, I'm just covering for a few hours. One of the crew's wife's pregnant, and he wanted to go to the scan."

"That's nice of you," Neal said with a smile.

"I'm a nice person most of the time," Delta said, smiling, and she couldn't believe she was almost flirting with Neal.

The ding for the elevator doors opening broke the moment, and Neal followed Delta inside. A month ago, she would've hyperventilated to be in a confined space with a man, but every time she saw Neal, she relaxed a little more around him.

The feeling obviously wasn't mutual because Neal started taking a few deep breaths.

"You okay?" Delta asked and without forethought, touched his shoulder.

Neal's clear blue eyes instantly met hers. Delta could feel the temperature rise in the elevator as her own heartbeat sped up, and this time it wasn't from fear.

Neal stepped back and nodded. "I'm fine, just still working

through some elevator-phobia."

Delta laughed as the elevator came to a stop on the ground floor. "Good luck with that, and with today."

As she walked out of the apartment building, she realized she had actually meant it when she wished him luck in court. Neal looked like a good guy, and sometimes good guys needed a little luck, especially when a bad guy was fighting dirty for the other side. Ever since she had told Neal she just wanted to be friends, he had kept his distance.

He was always friendly when he saw her, but in rare moments like this morning in the elevator, Delta knew whatever was breeding between them was soon going to peek out its head again. The fact that Neal hadn't mentioned it since that night gave her even more respect for him. Maybe one day she would be ready for what was growing between them, but for now, the easy greetings and harmless conversations worked fine.

She briskly walked towards the firehouse, enjoying the warmer morning. Winter was finally releasing its ice-cold grip and allowing some heat to seep into the dormant trees and flowers. Just yesterday, Delta had noticed the small potted plant on her balcony was starting to form a little bud. Just for that reason, she had poured herself a glass of wine. She had celebrated her little bud pushing through after the cold winter and couldn't help but equate herself with it. She was feeling more confident every day and didn't jump when a man came too close. She still struggled if they invaded her personal space or looked at her too long, but at least she was making some progress.

Smiling, she thought to herself that she, too, was pushing through the icy nightmare of months ago and starting to bloom again in Wilmington.

The firehouse was already a buzz of activity when Delta arrived; Michael Talbot, or Mike as he was called, sat with his coffee on the worn sofa with his feet on the scuffed coffee table and watched the morning news.

"Hey Mike," Delta called as she moved through the so-called waiting area, as Mike had introduced it to her. It was where the kitchen, the dining table, sofas, and the TV were stationed. Mike said they had dubbed it the waiting area since that was where they waited for their calls.

"Hey, Dee," Mike waved with one hand.

Various hellos were called her way from Yang, Beans, and Simmons. Delta smiled to herself as she made her way to her locker. For the first few weeks, all of the men in the firehouse had been standoffish with her, and then Mike started calling her Dee. Delta wasn't sure if it was the pet name, or if she had proven herself with the team, but finally, she didn't feel left out or talked about for being the only woman in the house.

During a late night chat, Beans had even revealed to her that everyone called him Beans because of his addiction to coffee.

After placing her satchel in her locker, she dressed in her uniform of trousers and a white shirt before going in search of coffee.

Delta had barely taken a sip of Bean's special brew when the alarm went off. In a flurry of movement that only firemen understood, the dance began. It was a sequenced ritual that appeared chaotic to anyone who wasn't used to being in a firehouse.

Feet slapped against the tile floors as the crew rushed to their suits. Within seconds, they had pulled on their fire retardant suits, boots, and helmets. Without consultation, everyone jumped into the truck. There wasn't time to fight over seats; everyone knew theirs by heart.

Within two minutes of the bell sounding, the truck and engine pulled out of the firehouse together, sirens wailing as they rushed towards the next call.

The usual adrenaline rush kicked in for Delta as her mind readied itself for what was to come. Lieutenant Kays called out the address and the situation in the usual tone he did with every call, only this time Delta's skin went ice cold, and the sharp gasp that followed it alerted Mike, who was sitting next to her.

"Dee, what's wrong?" He shook Delta's shoulder but got no response. "Guys, something's wrong with Dee!"

Lieutenant Kays turned around in his seat in the front and firmly said, "Eckhart!"

Delta forced herself to remain calm and looked Lieutenant Kays dead in the eye. "Could you please repeat the address?"

The lieutenant frowned but repeated the address again, meeting Delta's gaze when he finished. Delta took a deep breath and squared her shoulders. "That's my apartment."

The whole truck went quiet for about five seconds before everyone started talking together.

"Beans put your foot on the gas!"

"Are you sure?"

"Shit!"

"How bad is it?"

"Stop!" Lieutenant Kays said firmly and everyone kept quiet. "It's one of our own, so we need to make extra sure we keep our head in the game. No stunts, no mavericking!"

Everyone nodded, keeping their eyes on the road.

"Eckhart, I'm not letting you go in on this one; it's too personal."

"Lieutenant, at least can I go in for myself and assess the damage?"

Lieutenant Kays kept his eyes on Delta, and she knew he was searching for any emotion that would make her a risk. "We'll see when we get there."

The three miles to her apartment felt like they took forever. By the time they pulled up outside, there was already an audience watching the building burn.

From first assessment, Delta could tell it was only her apartment that was on fire. The windows overlooking the street from Neal's apartment were clear.

Everyone jumped out and waited for Lieutenant Kays to direct them. "Yang on ladder, Beans on hoses. The rest of you get inside and make sure there's nobody inside. Eckhart, you can join them if

Talbot takes responsibility for you." Both Lieutenant Kays and Delta turned to Talbot. Talbot nodded and pulled on his mask. "Come on, Eckhart."

Five firefighters rushed into the foyer, already knowing who was going up and working down and who was working from Delta's apartment down.

Delta's apartment on the sixth floor was burning, so there wasn't yet any smoke on the first few floors. Delta, Simmons, and Talbot were to head straight to her apartment and work back from there.

As they reached her floor, Delta was grateful to see the fire hadn't yet spread from her apartment. Talbot and Simmons turned around and shrugged. Delta understood immediately; they couldn't open her door, or they would risk the fire spreading.

She thought of the few things she had that mattered in that apartment; they weren't much, but still, they were the only things she had since leaving Craig. She was feeling emotion rush up and dim her vision when she felt Talbot's hand on her shoulder. "Go down, Dee, there's nothing you can do. We've got this."

Delta nodded and pushed the tears back as she made her way down the stairs again.

She heard the chief shouting orders, and her fellow teammates answering back in the distance. Delta closed her eyes and sat down on the foothold of the truck, pulling off her mask and helmet and watching as her apartment, only her apartment, went up in flames. The flames licked at the window frames as Yang blasted the hose directly into its ravenous mouth where Yang had broken the windows. That eerie sound that only a blazing fire made was the only sound Delta heard.

Just this morning, she felt positive about how she was pulling her life together: her friendship with Neal and her position at work. And here she was watching it all fall apart again.

Delta closed her eyes and backtracked through her steps that morning. She hadn't left anything on except the fridge. She had double-checked the windows and the locks on her door. The stove had been switched off the night before, so it couldn't be a gas leak. But if it wasn't any of those, what was it, and why was it her apartment?

An uncomfortable feeling sailed through her veins, making her glance over her shoulder. Like she thought, she didn't spot Craig in the crowd that was watching the fire burn, but there was one man who looked especially entranced by it. He was about six feet tall, wearing a long brown coat and a brown hat. His head was tilted towards her apartment, and if Delta didn't know better, she could swear he was smiling.

She stood up; wanting to ask him what was so funny, when Lieutenant Kays caught her by the arm. "You sit yourself down, Eckhart, where I can keep an eye on you, at least until this is over."

Delta nodded and took her seat on the foothold of the truck again. What had been an uncomfortable feeling before, now just felt completely off when the man with the brown coat and brown hat smiled in her direction before walking away.

Chapter 9

NEAL WAS STEPPING out of his office, ready to head to court, when he spotted his secretary standing with her hands over her heart, staring at the old box television in the corner of their small waiting area. The sight wasn't that troubling to Neal, who had worked with Ruth for over three years. Every time there was a report on greenhouse gases, an abandoned plant, or a puppy that had been run over, it seemed like the end of the world to Ruth.

Neal moved closer and placed a hand on the elderly woman's shoulder. It was as bony as Neal had suspected. Ruth had lived through three divorces and a son in jail and still was the only person that could run his office efficiently.

"What's going on, Ruth?" Neal asked and watched as the news reporter turned to the burning building behind her.

Ruth turned around and started to talk, "Isn't that..."

"That's my building!" Neal shouted as he took in the scene on the television. Firefighters were already on the scene that looked to be unfolding on Neal's floor. *Delta!* "Ruth, get someone to delay the hearing for me, I need to go," Neal said, even as he was running for the elevator.

Ruth snapped out of her grief-stricken stare and called after him, "Of course, you go on, Mr. Sullivan; I'll have it taken care of."

As Neal rushed the few blocks to his apartment, he wasn't certain if he was more worried that Delta was already back from work and caught in the blaze, or if she was still on duty and caught in the blaze.

The taxi driver sensed Neal's hurry and drove a little over the speed limit. By the time the taxi driver pulled up outside of Neal's building, the fire department had already doused most of the flames. Neal pushed through the crowd to get a better view of the building. Relief washed over him when he noticed his windows were intact; horror quickly replaced it when he noticed Delta's windows were broken, and acrid smelling smoke was drifting out the window and curling up towards the sky like a beast escaping as a firefighter on a ladder hosed even more water into the apartment.

Delta!

He rushed forward without thinking and nearly made it into the entrance before a large firefighter caught him by the arm.

"You can't go in, sir, not until the building is secured."

"But the woman, the woman that lives in that apartment…"

The large man loosened his grip on Neal's arm. "You mean Delta?"

"Yes, Delta - I'm not sure what her last name is."

"Delta Eckhart, she's over there by the truck. Not much we could do. We had to insulate her apartment to keep the fire from spreading. Chief's keeping an eye on her."

Neal turned around and noticed Delta sitting on the foothold of the truck with her helmet in her hand, staring up at her apartment.

His shoulders slowly relaxed, and his heart rate leaped before it slowed; later, he would ponder over both, but for now, he needed to make sure Delta was safe.

"Thanks," Neal said to the firefighter.

"Any time."

He walked with Neal towards Delta.

"Hey Dee, look what I found. Your beau's worried about

you."

Neal watched as the man affectionately ruffled Delta's hair.

"Buzz off, Mike!" Delta said to the retreating back of the other firefighter.

Neal knelt in front of her and took her face into his hands. For a moment, he noticed the brief flicker of fear in her eyes before they just looked despondent.

"Are you all right?" Neal asked in barely more than a whisper.

Delta sighed. "Well, physically I'm fine since I was barely allowed to help them fight it; otherwise, I've basically just lost everything I own. So I guess I'm not completely fine."

Without asking, Neal pulled her into a hug. It was awkward with the helmet still on her lap, but as soon as she rested her head against his shoulder, he felt her shoulders quiver.

"There now, it's going to be all right. I was so worried about you."

Delta pulled back, rubbing the moisture from her eyes before pegging Neal with eyes green as fresh cut grass. "Don't tell me it's going to be all right. Where am I going to live, what am I going to wear? Maybe sometime in the distant future it will be all right, but right now, it sucks."

Neal nodded, and Delta started saying something before stopping herself and frowning. He didn't prod; if she had something to tell him, she would do so in her own time.

"Neal!" At the sound of his name, Neal straightened up and saw the landlord Barry Williston hurrying towards him. "What on earth happened? I just saw on the news that my building is on fire?"

Neal knew Barry was prone to exaggeration, especially when it came to his real estate. "Calm down, Barry." He met Barry's eyes and continued, "No one was hurt; that is the most important thing."

Barry nodded as if it weren't before he rattled on. "What about the building, how bad is it? Oh, for goodness sake, Neal, what am I going to do?"

"Barry, like I said, the most important thing is no one was hurt, how about we wait for the firefighters to finish doing their job before we play worst-case scenario?"

From behind him, Neal heard a muffled smirk coming from Delta.

"Sure, sure." Barry's eyes flitted over the building a few times before looking past Neal at Delta still sitting in her spot. "Are you nearly done? When will I get a damage report?"

Delta smirked, and Neal noticed her eyes were flashing bright green again. Neal didn't know whether he stepped between them for Delta's sake or for Barry's safety.

"Barry, this is Delta Eckhart. It was her apartment that took the brunt of it."

Barry looked from Delta to Neal and back at Delta. Neal could almost hear the wheels spinning in his head, wondering if he was liable.

"I'm really sorry about the damage and your personal belongings, Ms. Eckhart. I want you to know I am insured, and you will be compensated for your losses."

"Will I be compensated with a new apartment?"

Neal had wondered the same thing and turned to Barry to hear his answer.

"Well, I'm not sure the insurance covers that... I might be able to spring for a motel until you find another place..."

"Isn't there any other apartment in the building vacant?" Delta asked.

"No unfortunately, this is my most popular building; that was the last one."

"Great, this is just darn great!" Delta sighed and pushed herself up before she moved towards the Chief. At least Neal assumed he was the Chief from the way he was directing the other firefighters.

"Neal, I don't know what to say. They don't even know what caused the fire yet; can they really make me provide her another place to stay?"

"Slow down, Barry, we'll sort something out."

Neal walked to Delta just as the other man spoke.

"It appears the building is structurally sound, but your apartment will require a lot of work. Mike or Yang can escort you to collect a few items... if there's anything left."

"Do you know what caused it?" Neal asked from behind Delta.

Delta turned around and gave him an irritated look. "Lieutenant Kays, this is Neal Sullivan, my neighbor. Neal, this is Lieutenant Kays."

Both men nodded before Lieutenant Kays spoke again. "Unfortunately, you'll have to wait for the report; I can't discuss any suspicions at this time."

"You'll have to wait for the report just like everyone."

Delta sighed and walked towards where Mike and Yang were waiting to escort her to her apartment. Neal watched her walk away, pushing the overwhelming relief that she was unharmed aside before he turned back to Barry who was peppering the lieutenant with questions.

Chapter 10

"DO YOU KNOW what caused it?" Delta asked both men at the same time. Both shrugged and followed Delta up to her apartment. The hallway outside her apartment was drenched, but luckily, it seemed Neal's apartment wasn't affected at all.

Delta took the key from her pocket and unlocked her apartment door. The scent of smoke and burnt plastic rushed over them as she took in the sight. Her comfortable couch was soaked and grey from the smoke and debris. The windows were shattered, and all her appliances partially or mostly melted. Delta quickly scanned the electric outlets and didn't notice any sign of the fire originating from them. She walked into her bedroom and hoped she still had clothes. There were black smoke marks climbing against the walls, and the bedding was a soaked jumble of rags pushed to the floor with the force of the hoses. Delta took a deep breath and tried to ignore the sight as she moved to her cupboard.

Right at the back of her cupboard there were a few dry items, even though the stench of smoke clung to them. Knowing now wasn't the time to be picky; Delta grabbed whatever she could, along with a few toiletries, and tossed it into the same duffel bag she had used six months ago. Yang took the bag from her as she walked through the apartment. There was nothing of sentimental value she wanted, she thought to herself, until she remembered one thing. She rushed out the balcony door and looked for her little budding plant; it lay scattered amongst the glass shards on the balcony, its soil littering the floor scattered and its tiny leaves bruised and beaten from the force of the water.

Delta was picking it up carefully, as if it were highly valuable crystal, when Mike's voice piped up.

"What've you got there?"

"My plant," Delta said.

"Out of everything in this apartment, you're worried about the plant?" Mike asked, confused.

Delta sighed. Even if she explained, Mike and Yang wouldn't understand; they wouldn't understand that the plant had been a symbol of her new life in Wilmington and that at the moment it felt as if her future depended on the plant surviving the fire and consequent force of water and glass.

She scanned her apartment one last time with Mike and Yang short on her heels and noticed the signature line of burned fuel running through her living room. Turning, she raised her brows as if to ask Mike and Yang if they noticed it.

Both men shrugged. "Delta, don't go jumping to conclusions, it could be nothing."

But Delta knew it wasn't. Her apartment had been torched, and no one would gain anything from doing it but Craig. An eerie shiver ran up her spine, and Delta remembered the man that had all but smiled at the fire before he walked away.

"Do I call the insurance company or the police? Neal, what should I do?"

Delta joined the two men where they were still standing by Lieutenant Kays. Barry was looking to Neal for direction; Neal was trying very hard to hide his irritability with the man.

"Delta, you got everything you need?" Lieutenant Kays asked as he spotted Delta.

Delta nodded. She didn't get everything, as most of it was burned to a crisp, but she did manage to get a few things.

"So what now?" Delta asked all three men, rattled after losing her home and most of her belongings.

"You can ride back with us, but only to get your things and to stash your gear. I'm sure you'll need a day or two to sort out new lodgings," Lieutenant Kays said with an air of authority.

"I can pay for a few nights in a motel until you manage to find somewhere else to stay." Barry looked at her with an awkward smile, and Delta knew he was hoping she'd say it wouldn't be necessary.

She felt Neal's hand on her elbow and looked up to meet his clear blue gaze. "Can I talk to you for a minute?"

Delta nodded and followed him away from the others.

"Barry can dock for a few nights in a motel, but that doesn't solve the problem. Where are you going to find a place for a few weeks? A motel is going to be expensive for the time it takes to fix your apartment, and it's no use getting a new apartment at this stage."

"Great, so you're basically telling me I'm screwed." Delta smiled wryly. "Such insight, really I can see now why you became a lawyer."

Delta knew she was being mean, but sarcasm at this stage was her only defense.

Neal clenched his jaw. "You're not completely screwed since I have a solution."

"What? You going to get Barry to move me into the basement?"

"No, I'm going to get you to move in with me."

Delta's eyes widened and blood rushed to her cheeks as she felt her fury rise. "What? Gee thanks, Neal, but I don't think our relationship has moved that far..." Delta turned to walk away, but Neal softly put a hand on her shoulder. She turned around, giving him a murderous glare.

"Delta, my apartment is much bigger than yours. We both work long hours and probably won't even be home the same times. I've got a spare bedroom with a lock on the door, if it helps. It just makes sense. That way you don't have to look for another apartment, you can be around to follow the renovation of your own apartment, and besides, you and I both know it wasn't a coincidence that just your apartment burned."

His eyes looked straight into hers like he was looking at her soul. For a moment, Delta could almost swear he knew about Craig. "I don't know what you mean," Delta said trying to defend herself.

"Delta, we don't know what happened yet, but when something like this happens, you let your friends help you."

Delta shrugged his hand off her shoulder. "I didn't know we were anything more than neighbors."

"We've shared two meals, Delta. In most circles, that would be regarded as friendship."

Delta wanted to refuse, she wanted to tell Neal to keep his nose out of her life, but he had a point. A motel would completely empty her savings account, a new apartment would be hard to find and expensive if she calculated in the deposit, even if Barry gave hers back. Besides, she liked her apartment and the building. It would only be a few weeks; how long could it take to fix her apartment?

Delta narrowed her eyes and stepped closer to Neal. "The door has a lock?"

"Yes, and you'll have the only key," Neal said firmly.

"No funny business?" Delta demanded.

Neal held up both his hands. "I promise."

Delta sighed and walked back to Barry and Lieutenant Kays. "Barry, Mr. Sullivan has been so kind to offer me a room until my apartment is done."

Barry clapped his hands together. "Neal! I knew you were a good man."

"Hold on, Barry, not so fast," Delta said, looking him straight in the eye. "Since you won't be paying my motel accommodation, I'll expect you to put a rush on fixing the apartment. As for the money you're saving on the motel, I'll expect a cash equivalent for inconvenience and to buy new furniture."

Barry gulped and nodded.

"Good, and lastly, I'm not paying rent until the apartment is livable again."

"Obviously." Barry nodded before turning to Neal. "She's a tough one, isn't she?"

Delta looked at Neal, who smiled almost proudly at her. "One of the toughest."

At his words, Delta felt flattered and felt a flicker of attraction tingle through her system.

Lieutenant Kays, who had listened to the whole exchange, turned to Barry. "Don't let anyone in until we've cleared it. Delta, let's go."

Delta nodded and was turning to walk to the truck when Neal called her back. "Leave your things; I'll take them up. So long."

Delta handed him her bag and the small plant she still held in her hand. "Just put it in some water, I'll deal with it when I get back."

Neal looked at the small plant in his hand and met her eyes, confused.

"Please," Delta said before jumping into the truck.

As the truck pulled away from the curb, Mike was the first to speak. "Lieutenant I think we should get arson to take a look at Eckhart's apartment."

Kays flicked his head around and frowned at Mike. "You see something off?"

"Me, Yang, and Eckhart did, Sir."

Kays turned towards Yang, who shrugged. "Looks like the place was torched, sir. Accelerant of some kind if you ask me."

Kays nodded before turning his eyes back on the road.

Delta wanted to kiss Mike and Yang for bringing it to Kays' attention. If she had, he would've thought she was foolish. The fact that they suspected the same as she did made her even more uncomfortable.

Why would someone torch her apartment? Even if she hated Craig, it wasn't his style. He would confront her and beat her if he ever found her, not burn her apartment down. No, something was off. The man in the brown trench coat and hat knew something, but there was no way to know who he was or how to find him.

Besides, if Delta knew anything about arson investigations, it was better to stay out of it before you got in the middle of it.

Chapter 11

NEAL FUSSED, AND he knew he was fussing, a task so foreign to him it made him irritable. He had opened the window in the spare bedroom to air it out, fresh linens were on the bed, and the plant Delta had handed to him with the greatest care sat on the chest of drawers, carefully planted in a small ceramic pot with the potting soil he had specially bought that afternoon. He had placed her duffel bag on the eighteenth century chest that stood by the foot of the bed and had debated even unpacking that for her.

He heaved a huge sigh and walked out of the room, shaking his head. *She's only staying for a few weeks, no need to get worked up about it.* But Neal knew exactly why he was worked up about it. It wasn't just any woman, it was Delta. The woman he couldn't get out of his mind since meeting her. He still didn't know why he had offered her a room, since he probably wouldn't get any sleep with her in his apartment. But he had made a promise and intended to keep it.

Whatever had put that look of fear in her eyes was the only thing that kept Neal from making a move again. If he didn't tread carefully, Delta would have him on his ass, and he wouldn't see her again. For some reason, that scared him; he didn't want to try and figure out why.

He walked into the kitchen and started poking in the fridge for ingredients to make dinner but found nothing worthwhile. It was late afternoon, and Delta still wasn't back from the fire station. The first two hours, Neal had been busy getting the room ready and catching up with some work. The next few hours, he had paced the apartment and checked the room a few times to make sure he didn't miss anything.

Now it was late afternoon, and Neal wondered if he shouldn't give her a call. No, he chastened himself. She wasn't his girlfriend, and he wasn't her keeper; she would come home when she was ready.

Home... the word set him on edge. He had never shared his home with anyone, and now he already thought of his apartment as Delta's home. He pulled a glass out of the cupboard and poured himself a glass of wine before opening his laptop; time was bound to go by faster if he focused on getting some work done.

Neal had just finished answering all his emails when there was a soft knock at the front door. He felt a nervous twitch in his belly and took a large gulp of wine before moving towards the door.

He opened the door, and Delta stood there looking bone-tired.

"Hi," she said with a foolish smile.

"You don't have to knock," Neal said, opening the door wider to let her in.

"I wasn't sure… I didn't want to be presumptuous," Delta said awkwardly before following him to the kitchen.

"Don't be stupid, you live here." Neal gave her a set of keys and pointed towards one. "That's for the bedroom, and the other's the front door."

Delta glanced at the keys in her hands and sat down on the stool beside the kitchen island. "Why are you doing this, Neal? We barely know each other."

Neal knew he could give a witty answer, but something in her eyes made him speak truthfully. "I don't know why, but I have a feeling you've had it rough and could do with a hand and a friend right about now."

Delta smirked and made it obvious she wasn't about to confirm or deny his statement. "Can I have some wine?" The smirk and the look in her eye told Neal he wasn't too far from the truth.

"Sure." He poured a glass of red wine and handed it to her.

"We probably need to talk about rent, groceries, chores, and the other stuff that goes with living together."

Neal narrowed his eyes at her before moving around the island and sitting down beside her. "I didn't offer you a room to get you to clean and cook for me, Delta."

"Still, I'm not staying if I can't contribute," Delta said resolutely.

"Fine, if you're going to be stubborn about it. We both clean up after ourselves, if you do cook it would be nice if you leave me a plate, same goes for me. As for groceries, I don't really stock the fridge unless I'm planning to cook; if you want to, I promise I won't use your things."

Delta laughed. "Really? You're letting me stay here for free, and you're worried about drinking my milk?"

Neal shrugged. "Let's just see how it goes. We're both adults; if something isn't working, we can sort it out."

"Fair enough," Delta said sipping on her wine.

"Rough day? I thought you'd be back sooner?" Neal asked, knowing he was probing.

"We had to debrief and then the arson investigator came by."

"Arson?" Neal asked, hoping his suspicions weren't right.

"Yes, Mike, Yang and I noticed some form of accelerant line running through my living room."

"So in layman's words, that would mean…"

"Either I dropped a can of gasoline in my living room or someone torched the place."

A protective gene in Neal awoke for the first time in his life; he laid his hand over Delta's. "You mean…"

"Yes, it looks like arson."

"Shit! Now I'm even more relieved you agreed to stay here."

"Why?" Delta asked, confused.

"Because no one is going to hurt you while you're staying with me."

Delta laughed. "Neal, who said they were trying to hurt me? It could've been some kids, a random torching by a juvenile arsonist. There's no way to know if this had anything to do with me."

"Still, I feel better knowing you're staying here."

With their heads close together and Neal's hand still on

Delta's, the air thickened. She smelled like soap and the mysterious essence of woman. Nothing had ever attracted Neal more. With her tired eyes focused on his, Neal wanted nothing more than to lean closer and to lay his lips against hers. But he had made a promise.

He briskly stood up and fetched his phone from the charger. "There isn't really anything to cook for dinner, and to be honest, I don't feel like cooking. Chinese, pizza, or burgers?"

Delta swallowed, and Neal knew the moment had affected her as much as him. "Didn't you go back to work?"

"No. I missed court this morning, so I worked from home the rest of the day."

Delta nodded before pursing her lips. "Pizza, definitely pizza."

"Pepperoni, cheese, and pineapple?" Neal asked as he dialed the number.

"Pepperoni, olives, chili, and extra cheese," Delta said, smiling, and her tummy roared loudly. "And tell them to hurry."

Neal laughed and placed the order.

They ate pizza at the kitchen island with a second glass of wine. Again, Delta surprised Neal by matching him slice for slice.

Even though the chilies burned through the roof of his mouth, he had to admit it was delicious. They talked about non-consequential things like the weather and Neal's choice of furnishings. Neal had made sure to keep his distance and not to touch all through dinner. He wasn't sure if it was for Delta's benefit or because he was afraid if he got too close again he wouldn't be able to pull back.

By the time the box of pizza was empty, Delta stood up. "If you show me the room, I think I'm going to unpack and have an early night."

Neal rose with her and led her to the spare bedroom.

Delta walked in and scanned the room. Neal shuffled uncomfortably, hoping he didn't miss anything, as Delta moved towards the chest of drawers. "You planted it?"

"What?" Neal asked, confused, still wondering if he missed something.

"My plant? You planted it?" Neal could almost swear there were tears glistening in her eyes.

"Yes, it didn't seem right to just toss in some water. I went to the nursery and the lady told me the ceramic pot would be good to keep in moisture, and she gave me some kind of potting soil that nourishes sick and hurt plants."

Delta rushed towards him, and just when Neal was sure she was going to hug him, she pulled back and said reservedly, "Thank you."

"My pleasure," Neal said, wondering why the plant meant more to her than the fresh linens.

Delta looked around and met his eyes again. "Can I maybe have a towel?"

Neal shook his head. "I knew I missed something." He opened the closet and pulled a fresh fluffy bath sheet from the top shelf. "Here you go. I emptied some closet space for you, let me know if you need more."

"Thank you."

Neal wasn't sure if it was because he was trying to keep his hands off her, or if it was the frightened look in her eyes whenever he came close, but his temper was on edge when he spoke. "Can you just stop thanking me? It's just a room."

He noticed a smile tug at the corner of her mouth. "Sure. Good night, Neal."

"Night, bathroom is just across the hall."

"I figured," Delta said, smiling at him.

Neal stood for another minute looking at her before she raised her brows, and he realized she was waiting for him to leave.

He went back to the kitchen and rinsed their glasses before trying to get in some more work. Delta's presence made focusing nearly impossible. He heard the water start to run when she took her bath, heard her door close and the lock turn when she headed back to her room, and wondered how he was going to spend a few weeks living with a woman who had crept under his skin without even trying.

Neal woke in the middle of the night for about the fifth time. Every time, he woke restless and wondering if Delta was asleep or restless like he was. He grabbed his bottle of water from the bedside table, only to find it empty. With a curse, he pushed up and headed to the kitchen to grab another bottle. He stopped briefly in front of Delta's closed door before moving away.

He stepped into the kitchen and couldn't help but wonder if he was dreaming or having a hallucination. In the soft light coming from the fridge, Delta stood wearing only a t-shirt and short flannel pants skimming the top of her thighs, assessing the contents.

Her legs were long, toned, and smooth. From his vantage

point, he noticed the perfect curve from her thigh to her rear and was aching to reach out and touch it when Delta turned and all but jumped.

"Shit! You scared me," she said with a sleepy laugh.

"Sorry, I didn't know you were up," Neal said, realizing he was standing there in his boxers.

He watched as Delta's eyes took their time travelling over his bare torso before reaching his eyes.

"Couldn't sleep," she said before biting her lower lip.

Neal felt his breath back up and clenched his fists to keep them from reaching for her. "Neither could I. I just came to get some water."

Delta reached into the fridge and passed him a bottle of water. Their hands barely touched, but that touch was enough for Neal to know keeping his hands off Delta was going to be easier said than done.

He heard Delta gasp at the touch and met her sleepy gaze. "Delta…" his words were barely more than a whisper.

Delta ran her tongue unconsciously over her lower lip, "Neal…"

Neal watched her chest rise and fall as her breath sped up and knew he was in trouble. He moved a fraction closer and noticed her sleepy gaze quickly transform into fear.

Stepping back, he kept his eyes on hers. "No funny business, I promise."

Delta nodded and closed the fridge, leaving them standing in the dark.

Neal sensed her moving closer and wanted nothing more than to take her in his arms, but sensibility prevailed.

He took a step back and said into the darkness, "Good night, Delta."

Without waiting for her answer, he turned and headed to his bedroom, where he knew he wasn't going to get a minute's sleep for the rest of the night.

Chapter 12

"With broken wings

We stand together

Like birds of a feather.

We now know we do not lack,

And we can FIGHT BACK!"

DELTA WAS BENDING to pick up her satchel at her feet when she heard Nadine's voice over her shoulder. "So how's the new friend?"

Delta smiled into Nadine's molten chocolate-brown eyes and answered teasingly, "Great, I moved in with him."

Delta couldn't help but laugh at Nadine's expression.

"Girl, I've never been one to say this, but aren't you moving too fast?" Nadine's eyes were as concerned as her voice was shocked.

"No, but it's a long story. Do you have time for coffee?" Delta checked her watch to confirm she had time. It was an hour before her shift started at 8 p.m., and she hoped Nadine had some time.

"Sure, girl. Besides, there're few things I like better than a long story."

After both Delta and Nadine sat down at a table in the corner with their coffee, Delta filled Nadine in on everything that had happened since they last spoke.

"And I thought I had a rough week!" Nadine shook her head as she placed a hand over Delta's. "So was it arson?"

"The arson investigators are still busy, or if they do know, they're not telling me."

"And how's it going living with Neal, are you managing?"

Delta shrugged. She wasn't about to tell Nadine about how she had knots in her belly every time she unlocked Neal's apartment, and they weren't from fear. They were little bundles of excitement, bursting to see Neal. "Yes, he gave me a key to lock my bedroom door."

"That was nice. Did you tell him about Craig?"

Delta frowned. "No, I didn't. I think he knows that without the key, I wouldn't have accepted his offer."

"Sounds like a nice man, your new friend." Nadine winked and Delta laughed.

"We are just friends, Nadine, no funny business."

"Honey, men and woman can't just be friends. Haven't you learned that?"

"I beg to differ," Delta said resolutely. "I have a bunch of male friends at work, and things have never been awkward between us."

"Male colleagues, Delta. There is a big difference." Nadine widened her eyes to drive the point home before she spoke again. "Well, honey, I'm gonna say it again, if you're interested in Neal, you're over the man fast, but just be careful."

"I will be. How are things on your end?" Delta asked, wanting to learn more about Nadine.

"Nothing new, besides I'm not paying attention to the man that sends me flowers twice a week and asks for my number every time."

"A man?"

"Yes, I met him at the diner where I wait tables. He's convinced I'm the girl he's going to marry."

"Wow, that's..." At a loss of words, Delta just raised her

brows. "…eager of him."

"Hell, this man is so eager, he frightens me half to death, and his sunny disposition frightens me even more."

Delta had to laugh. Nadine had made it clear previously she was attracted to men with troubled souls. "Maybe his sunny disposition is just what you need."

"Ha!" Nadine huffed.

"Maybe you should become friends, that way you'll learn to trust him first." Delta repeated Nadine's own words.

"You did not just throw my own words back at me!"

"Of course I did," Delta smiled. "They were good words."

Nadine laughed from her belly, and Delta joined in. It felt good to have a friend to laugh with again.

"I need to hurry; my shift starts in a few, but we'll talk more next week?" Delta said, standing up.

"Sure, as long as you don't boomerang my own words again." Nadine winked at Delta before pulling her in for a brisk hug.

The simple act had Delta's throat clogging with emotion. "Thanks."

"For what?" Nadine said as she released Delta.

"For being a good friend," Delta said honestly.

"Anytime, sugar. See you soon." With that, Nadine left the group in a flurry of hugs and waves, and Delta couldn't help but think she had found a great friend in Nadine.

When Delta walked into Neal's apartment the following evening just after eight, she was bone-tired and emotionally drained. She had just locked the door behind her when she heard Neal's voice.

"Delta, what happened?" Neal moved towards her from where he was working at the dining room table. The table was a scattered mess of papers, notes, and different color pens.

"Wow. I knew I felt bad, I didn't realize I looked it." Delta dropped her keys and satchel on the kitchen island.

"I didn't mean that...well, I did but..." Neal fumbled before finally scratching his head, at a loss for words.

"Its okay, Neal; it was just a rough day," Delta said moving into the kitchen, where she noticed Neal had covered a plate for her.

Neal took out two glasses and poured them each a glass of wine. "Want to talk about it?"

"No, it's fine; I can see you're busy," Delta said taking a bite of spaghetti. "Aaah, you've so done enough! This was just what I needed!" The spaghetti was salty with a slight zing of tomato and hit the spot perfectly.

"I'm not busy. Well, I don't have to be, and I'd like to know what happened. This is the first time after a shift I can see something happened."

Delta laughed dryly. "Well actually, a few things happened."

"So start at the first," Neal suggested as he sat down beside her, giving her his full attention.

Delta chewed on another bite of spaghetti before she sighed and turned to Neal. "When I got to work last night, Mike gave me a heads up about the arson investigation."

"They're making progress?" Neal asked.

"No, they're looking at the wrong person."

"Who?"

"Me."

"What?"

"Yup, Mike told me last night that since it's my apartment and it was arson, the first point of investigation is me. Especially since the fire was reported barely an hour after I arrived at the station."

"That's ridiculous!" Neal said vehemently.

"Actually, it isn't." Delta sighed. "If you look at the timeline, it could be probable, and firefighters are on occasion arsonists. But they're missing the bigger picture: why would I burn down my own apartment? Heck, if I was an arsonist, why not burn down the whole building?"

"What did you do?"

"Nothing, since it won't help if I interfere. I'd only look more suspicious."

"So you're not going to do anything about being their main suspect?"

"Nope. Besides, Mike had just dropped the bomb before we were called out to a residential fire."

"I heard something about it on the news this morning, were you there?"

"Yes," Delta said, eating a little more, giving herself time to process the night emotionally before telling Neal.

"The woman?" Neal asked softly.

A tear slipped from her eye at Neal's words. "When we got there, it was bad, Neal. I mean, like real bad. We had almost zero visibility when we entered the place. It was an electrical fire in the basement, and we struggled through the smoke and flames to find them. After about ten minutes, we found the man in the living room passed out behind the couch. We got him out just in time before the house blew. We didn't have time..." Delta couldn't control the emotion anymore. The tears she never shed at the station now poured freely as her shoulders racked from the sobs.

Neal's strong arms pulled her close until her head was nestled in the crook of his neck.

"We didn't know..." Delta sobbed. "The man was unconscious; we couldn't even ask him..."

"Shhh, there now... You did everything you could," Neal soothed as his hand gently stroked her hair.

"But if we had searched again, or maybe started in a different room..." Delta whispered against his neck through the tears.

"You might've missed the man..." Neal let the words hang between them as Delta cried for a woman who had died a cruel death at the hands of a ravenous fire.

Never before had Delta thought she would need to be consoled after a fire, but last night was different. When they did the walk through and found the woman hiding under the bed, burned beyond recognition, Delta had to swallow her emotion and deal with the practicalities. The neighbor, a woman in her late thirties, had collapsed when they had to tell her that her neighbor didn't survive the fire. Delta was trying to console the woman when she told Delta about the wonderful people Pete and Ursula Smith were. Pete was the loving, faithful husband, and Ursula had just found out she was having their first baby after they had been trying for a year.

Delta couldn't get herself to mention that part to Neal because that was the part that had devastated Delta. Pete had just lost his wife, his house, and his unborn child.

By the time the tears had subsided and her breathing had returned to normal, Delta realized Neal was still holding her. She quickly scanned her mental state and realized she wasn't scared; she felt safe in his arms.

She drew away slowly and smiled at him sheepishly. "Your shirt is wet."

Neal smiled and used his thumb to wipe a tear from her eye. "It'll dry." His thumb trailed to her swollen lips and softly rubbed over them.

Delta's gaze drifted from Neal's eyes to his lips and couldn't help but wonder what kind of a lover he would be. Would he be gentle and patient, or would he be rough and demanding? She had a feeling that, when given the choice, Neal would be both demanding and patient in equal measures.

The sadness of her shift and the worry over the arson investigation fled from her mind as Neal's eyes, blue as the Caribbean, met hers. The soft flicker of attraction that had haunted her since their first meeting became a flashing light beckoning her to take a chance. Delta wanted with all her heart to believe Neal was different from Craig, but was he? What guarantee did she have that Neal wouldn't turn to violence when a case wasn't going his way?

The memory of the pain and shame of her last night with Craig leaked into her mind like a thick fog, making everything else disappear.

She inched her head back, and Neal dropped his hand, waiting for her to make the first move. Delta wanted to appreciate the gesture but couldn't help but wonder if that was just another tactic men used. If you made the first move, it was your fault, wasn't it?

A dull throb started beating at the base of her skull. She wasn't sure if it was exhaustion or sensory overload from having Neal so close, but she needed to get away.

Delta stood up and pushed the half-eaten plate of spaghetti

aside. "I'm going to have a bath and head to bed."

Neal watched her, the question clear in his eyes. Did she feel it too?

"I'm sorry," Delta whispered under her breath as she grabbed her keys and satchel and all but ran for her room.

As soon as she slammed the door shut behind her, she realized staying away from Neal was going to be harder than she had initially thought. There was something between them brewing slowly. It was mysterious and hypnotic, and soon it would reach boiling point. Delta could only hope she would be ready to make a choice when it did.

Chapter 13

"MR. SULLIVAN, ARE you ready to deliver your closing statement?" The judge, a man in his late sixties, peered at Neal over half-moon glasses.

"Yes, your honor." Neal stood up and looked at the prepared statement in front of him before turning to Denise Ascot, the victim. The courthouse smelled of nervous sweat and bated breath.

On a whim, he closed the file with the prepared statement and spoke from the heart, something Neal rarely did in court.

"Members of the jury, over the past week, you have heard both sides of a story. A story that was meant to be one of love, but turned into something dark and painful for Mrs. Ascot. Yes, I agree that Mrs. Ascot should've reported every time her husband physically abused her; I also agree that she should've reported the times he raped her. But I ask you this: can you blame a woman for being too ashamed, too abused by her own husband to report the vile things that occurred during her marriage? I applaud Mrs. Ascot for her courage in reporting the final assault and rape she was subjected to, even if the defense says it isn't enough. Do you believe that? Do you believe that giving a statement of seven years of abuse and rape, being psychologically evaluated by both parties, and having to repeatedly tell her story is not enough? I beg to differ. I think Denise Ascot deserves to be acknowledged for coming forward. For facing the shame and accusations that go with it. Yes, the medical report stated there were no signs of forced entry that indicated that the sex could've been consensual, but was it? What would Mrs. Ascot gain from lying about this? Her husband isn't an affluent man that can afford to pay her alimony. Mrs. Ascot just asks for justice. She wants justice for the seven years she endured of being beaten and raped repeatedly by the man who promised to love and protect her. Yes, she didn't report each beating, but I believe that the x-ray evidence is enough to convince you of the fact that over the past seven years, she has broken her wrist, her collarbone, her jaw, and, last but not least, three ribs. Either Mrs. Ascot is a very accident-prone woman," Neal paused and turned to look at Mrs. Ascot, who sat with her head held high even though tears were streaming from her eyes, "or she is telling the truth. I trust you've heard enough to know what the truth is and that you will consider the hell Mrs. Ascot has faced over the past seven years before reaching a verdict."

"Thank you, Mr. Sullivan," the judge said before slamming his gavel twice.

"The jury will now go into session; you will be contacted when a verdict has been reached."

"Thank you," Denise Ascot said to Neal before leaving the courtroom.

Neal gathered his things and left the courthouse. By the time he unlocked his apartment door, he was tired, agitated, and wanted nothing more than a cold beer. The sight that met him was even better.

Delta was dancing to Elle King blaring from the speakers of his surround system in the kitchen. Her hips swayed with the beat as she shook some salt over a casserole dish. Her hair was loose, bouncing on her shoulders with the movement. A tight shirt in bright green hugged her torso, just as the denim shorts hugged her hips before fraying at the edges mid-thigh. Barefoot, she sang along, lost in the song; she swiveled around and came to a brisk stop when she spotted Neal.

"Hi!" Delta shouted over the music before grabbing the remote and turning it down. "Sorry, I didn't expect you back till much later."

Her eyes were bright and her cheeks a rosy red as she smiled at him. Neal felt the heavy day start to melt away. "I'm done in court, the jury is in session. Didn't feel like heading back to the office."

"Oh," Delta said, tilting her head, confused.

Over the two weeks since she'd moved in with him, Neal had shared very little of his career with Delta. The few times he did, a somber look came into her eyes, and she promptly rushed to her room. Since she stood there watching him, Neal tugged his tie loose and decided to tell her a little more. "I just delivered the final statements for the case we were working on."

"Is that a good thing?" Delta asked, picking up a bottle of sparkling water and screwing off the lid.

"Depends. In some ways it's good because it's finished, and in some ways it's bad because now it's done. There's nothing you can do to change the verdict. You can only hope what you did was enough."

Delta nodded and slipped the casserole dish into the oven before turning back to him. "Beer or wine?"

"What are you having?" Neal asked, glancing at the water bottle.

"Neither, I'm giving my kidneys a wash." She laughed at her words and took another sip of water. Living with her had taught Neal that Delta rarely enjoyed a glass of wine, and when she did, she had only once had more than one.

"Beer, then." Neal shrugged out of his coat and placed it neatly over a dining room chair before heading to the fridge for a beer. Once the top was uncapped, he took a long drink and sighed.

"Want to talk about it?" Delta asked, moving into the living room. "The chicken casserole is going to take at least another hour, if you'd like to blow of some steam."

She folded both her feet underneath her and watched Neal expectantly.

"Delta, I don't know if I should. Every time I mention the word lawyer or case, you freeze up."

Delta pursed her lips and thought for a moment before smiling at him. "You know what, you're right. But you keep saying you're one of the good guys, so why don't you tell me what a good guy lawyer did in court today?"

Neal knew he shouldn't, but he needed to talk about it. If Delta wasn't staying with him, he would've gone by his parents to talk it over before coming home. *Well, she did offer*, he reasoned before sitting down beside her. "The case I had…it wasn't pretty."

"I can handle that, not a lot of things in my line of work are pretty."

"Fair enough. Right, where to begin? Denise Ascot has been married for seven years, during which her husband repeatedly raped and abused her. She didn't report any of the beatings or rapes because she was too ashamed. When he raped and beat her the last time, she packed her bags and asked a friend to drive her to hospital. After the rape kit was taken and all the necessary medical tests were done, she made a case against him for rape and assault."

Delta's eyes widened, and Neal watched as she swallowed before breathing deeply.

"Delta, if it's too much, I'll stop."

"No, first tell me this: whom did you represent?"she asked, narrowing her eyes.

Neal shook his head as if it were a rhetorical question. "Denise Ascot."

Delta nodded firmly before smiling at Neal. "Good, now tell me what you did to make sure she gets justice."

"Well since the rape kit didn't show any sign of forced entry, it was hard to demonstrate rape. So I motivated it with the fact that after being repeatedly raped, she knew the beatings would be less severe if she cooperated."

"Which doesn't make it consensual?"

"Exactly. From the scans and x-rays, we were able to argue that she had multiple fractures over the past seven years, all of which point towards physical abuse. Before her marriage, she had never suffered a single fracture. When she had arrived at the hospital the last time, she had broken ribs and bruises on her face, so that backed up the last rape."

"Point for you," Delta said holding her water up in a salute.

"Thanks. So basically we argued that society makes it hard for a woman to report abuse of any kind, as there is usually a stigma attached that they were asking for it. We also had a psychologist who had interviewed her numerous times confirm the fact that she had been a victim of long-term domestic abuse. Now I can only hope I did enough."

Delta stood up and knelt in front of Neal. "I might've had an idea, but now I know you're a good guy."

Neal froze as her hands rested on his knees, her face a few inches from his own. He could smell her floral fragrance mingled with soap. He wanted to touch her but was afraid any movement would scare her away.

Delta slowly inched forward until her lips were against his. The touch was soft at first, almost tentative, exploratory. Neal felt her sigh against his lips before she turned her head and took the kiss to the next level.

As Delta swept into his mouth, the furnace that had been simmering for weeks started to hiss and spark with new life. Her lips were soft and her tongue demanding as it dueled with is. Neal angled his head to deepen the kiss even more and tasted exactly what he was hoping to find.

Desire.

There were a few things you could lie about, but you couldn't lie about desire when you were kissing someone. Neal could taste it on her tongue, could feel it in the pressure of her lips against his; he didn't just imagine it.

Wanting more, Neal slid his hand into her hair, pulling her close.

Delta moaned into his mouth at the touch, and Neal nearly became undone. When had she bewitched him so?

Her tongue glided roughly against his, and Neal couldn't stop the groan that escaped. Delta went stiff against him and pulled back. The split second Neal had to see her eyes before she jumped up and ran out, he noticed the frightened look in them.

The door slammed shut, its echo travelling through the house to Neal where he still sat confused on the couch. He wiped a hand over his brow and checked the time on his watch; the casserole would almost be ready.

After a restless night of sleep, Neal was woken by his phone just after seven a.m. Delta had never left her room last night, and after debating whether or not to bring her food, Neal had decided it was best to leave her be. He had spent the whole night tossing and turning with their kiss haunting his mind. The few moments his mind wasn't spinning over Delta, he wondered what the jury would decide.

He picked up his phone and answered it gruffly. "Sullivan."

"Jury's in."

Neal set the phone down and jumped out of bed. It was done, he tried to convince himself as he briskly showered and prayed for a miracle. He had just exited the apartment building when his phone rang again.

"Sullivan," he barked for the second time that morning.

"Sullivan here," Caleb repeated.

"Hey, Caleb."

"Hey yourself. I hear you're a regular attention seeker these days. Didn't get enough of it as golden boy growing up?" Caleb teased.

"What?" Neal asked, confused, as he hailed a cab to the courthouse.

"Mom and Dad told me about the fire."

"Oh, that," Neal said, climbing into the cab that had pulled up beside him. He rattled off his destination before listening to Caleb again.

"Is your apartment okay?"

"Yeah, it was my neighbor's apartment. Luckily, nothing else suffered damage."

"Your new neighbor?"

"Yes."

"Since you're on your way to court, I'll make this quick. Mom says she moved in with you?"

Neil sighed. "Really? This family grapevine thing really gets on my nerves."

"Well, it's your family, too; besides, we're just worried about you."

"About what? She needed a place to stay; I have a room, problem solved."

"Right, and how about the fright-and-flight mode you spoke about last time?"

"I don't know, Caleb. I said I thought there was an attraction, and when I acted on it, she looked frightened."

"Fine, that then. Are you still attracted to her now that you're living together?"

"Really, I don't have time for this."

"Actually you do, because if you were in court already, you would've hung up by now, which mean you're still on your way."

"Fine, yes."

"Is she still scared?"

Neal sighed and briefly told Caleb about what had happened the night before. The line was quiet for a while until Caleb finally spoke. "Neal, this really sounds strange. I think you'd better leave her alone. What if she slaps you with a sexual harassment suit or something? She sounds confused to say the least."

Neal thought it over. "You're wrong. I agree she's confused, but something's happened to her Caleb, I just don't know what."

"Then either you find out or you kick her out. You've never been a sucker for punishment."

Neal heaved a heavy sigh as the taxi pulled up in front of the courthouse. "I'll think about it. I've got to go."

He hung up the phone and got out of the taxi, thinking about Caleb's words. Maybe he was right. Neal needed to either find out what was going on or leave her alone because the hot and cold signals she was sending were a recipe for disaster.

Chapter 14

"MISS ECKHART, HAVE you ever been fascinated with fire?" the stern woman sitting across from Delta asked accusingly. Half-moon spectacles were balanced on her nose, and her eyebrows were drawn taught by the tight bun on top of her head.

"Yes, since I was a child and my father was a fire-fighter," Delta answered knowing the answer could be construed to implicate her.

"Have you ever set a fire?"

Delta smiled wryly. "Look, let me do us both a favor and cut to the chase. I know what you're doing. You're trying to assess whether or not I have pyro tendencies. Well, I can assure you I don't. I've always been fascinated at the speed with which a fire can turn, and how to outsmart it. I've never been fascinated by the death and havoc it causes. I didn't set the fire in my apartment. You can check my file; I've never shown any tendencies in that direction."

Half-moon spectacles were lowered to reveal narrowed eyes under a cocked brow.

Delta held up her hand. "Before you say it, I know there is a first time for everything. But I can assure you I didn't do it, and at least give me some credit. If I started the fire, I wouldn't have used something as obvious as fuel in the center of the living room. I'm a firefighter; I can think of much more inventive ways."

"Miss Eckhart, I understand you're bothered by this investigation, but it is necessary. Your cooperation would be appreciated."

"I am cooperating. I've sat here for the last hour explaining what happened that morning, and if after the past hour you still think I set the fire, I don't think there is anything I can do to convince you otherwise."

"I never said you set…"

"You didn't have to. The fact that I'm being formally interviewed by the head arson investigator says it all."

The bell rang out loudly, and Delta breathed a huge sigh of relief. "Now if you'll excuse me, I've got a fire to put out!"

Delta shoved the chair back and stood up. After donning her gear and jumping into the truck, she breathed deeply a few times to calm herself. She needed her full focus before stepping into the fire.

For the past week, she had been doing a lot of deep breathing, Delta thought as the truck wailed out of the station. Between her restless nights thinking about Neal and worrying over the arson investigation, restful sleep had been scarce.

Since she ran out on Neal after their kiss, they had come to what Delta thought of as silent stale-mate. They were friendly but not too friendly. All physical contact had ceased, and Neal rarely looked her in the eye, something that bothered her endlessly. She felt attracted to Neal: to his personality, his smile, and the way she felt when he was around. She just didn't know how she was going to stop her body from jumping to flight mode whenever Neal touched her.

"We're here," Lieutenant Kays said as the truck stopped in the middle of Cape Fear Memorial Bridge.

Delta frowned and was looking out the window searching for the fire when she spotted him. A man had climbed over the barricades and was standing at the edge of the bridge. The fire department rarely got called out on suicide attempts, but when they did, Delta knew it was always a sensitive situation. You literally had that person's life in your hands and only your words to coax them back.

Lieutenant Kays and Mike were standing to the side of the truck debating over which one of them should approach the man to talk him down when Delta joined them.

"Let me go." Both men turned to her, confused.

"Eckhart, this is a sensitive situation. I'm not sure you're equipped…" Lieutenant Kays said before turning back to Mike.

Delta glanced towards the man and noticed his shoulders were shaking as he sobbed.

"Lieutenant, do you know who that man is?" Delta said in a tone a little more harsh than she intended.

"What?" he asked, confused.

"That is Pete Mitchell. We pulled him out of his burning house last week; his wife didn't make it." Delta knew she was bordering on insubordination, but she'd been smacked around enough the past few years; this morning just topped it all off.

Both men turned their full attention to Delta. "Are you sure?" Mike asked.

"I'm sure. Please let me go talk to him. I'll strap in and won't go too close unless it's necessary," Delta begged. She needed to do something. Her life was spinning out of control; hopefully, she could help Pete to keep his together.

Mike and Kays shared a glance before they both turned to Delta. "You strap in, and if at any moment I feel it's not working, you get back here when I call."

"Understood." Delta ran over to the truck and strapped into the harness before slowly making her way over the barricades. She stopped about six feet from Pete on the dangerous side of the guardrail.

"Hello Pete, do you remember me?" Delta asked softly, as if she was speaking to a wounded animal.

Pete turned to look at her and nodded. "You were there. You pulled me out."

"That's right, Pete. I was there, and I know it wasn't your fault." Delta made the mistake of glancing down towards the water and felt her stomach contents lurch.

"It was! If I had checked those damn electricity lines, I could've prevented the whole thing."

"Pete, it was a short on the wiring in the wall. Nothing you could've prevented. It wasn't your fault." It was a white lie, but right now Pete needed one. Delta pursed her lips and searched for the wife's name. "Ursula wouldn't want you to blame yourself."

Another sob racked the man's shoulders as a fresh wave of tears streamed over his face. "I buried them this morning. Do you know what it's like to bury your wife and your unborn baby?"

Emotion clogged her throat, and she took a moment to swallow it down before speaking. "No, I don't, but I do know that she loved you very much. Your neighbor told me what a good husband you were to Ursula and how much she loved you. She wouldn't want this. She would want you to cherish your memories together and to remember her as you continue living your life for both of them."

Pete inched forward, and Delta held her breath; she knew the rest of the crew would rush forward at any second so she held up her hand.

"Pete, if you're jumping, you're not jumping alone."

That got his attention. He stepped back from the edge and looked at Delta. "Why would you jump?"

"Because I feel the same way you do. If we had gotten there seconds sooner, if we had searched faster…"

"It's not your fault; you were wonderful, the way you pulled me out…"

"Thank you, Pete, but that's just it, isn't it? We all did the best we could; you passed out from smoke inhalation because you didn't want to stop searching for her."

"I couldn't - I couldn't leave her there."

"I know, Pete, and she knows it, too. I know it's hard, but Ursula wouldn't want you to kill yourself. She would want you to live a long, happy life."

"She always teased that if something should happen to her, I should get another wife so someone else could understand how annoying I am." A hint of a smile tugged at his mouth.

"Exactly. She wouldn't want you to jump; she'd want you to annoy your next wife." Delta tried to smile but struggled.

"But I can't. I don't want another wife. I want Ursula." Pete edged forward again.

"Pete, you don't have to get another wife right this minute; no one expects that. You need time to grieve for your wife and for your baby, but jumping off this bridge won't solve it."

Delta took off her helmet and unhooked the harness from the rope. Pete watched her and gasped. "What are you doing?"

"You jump, I jump. Remember?" Delta said, even as she heard Kays shouting her name in the background.

Keeping one hand on the guardrail, Delta inched towards Pete, holding out her hand. "So what's it going to be?"

Pete glanced at the river below and back at Delta before looking down at the river again. He brushed away the tears, and Delta held her breath, waiting for him to jump.

"I think I'll try grieving a little. I'm not fond of water."As Pete's palm slammed against Delta's and she felt his fingers close around her hand, she tugged him towards the guardrail. Within seconds, Simms, Yang, and Beans were hanging onto both of them and helping them over the guardrail.

When they were both safe, Pete took Delta's hand. "She would've liked you."

Delta smiled and squeezed Pete's hand. "I'm sure I would've liked her, too."

The medics escorted Pete to hospital to be checked out, and Delta returned to the truck, expecting Kays to start breathing fire any minute because she had unhooked herself. Instead he smiled at her and slapped her on the shoulder. "Great work, Eckhart, we're grateful to have you on the team." Congratulations were passed around freely as all the men on the team took a turn shaking Delta's hand.

Delta smiled as the warm feeling of acceptance washed over her. Everything else might be falling apart in her life, but at least at work things were going right.

Delta had just finished taking a shower before heading home when her phone buzzed in her pocket. She pulled it out and couldn't help but smile at the message.

Don't go to sleep yet. Will be home soon with pizza.

N

The message wasn't flirty. It was simply kind, and it was with his kindness that Neal had started to make room for himself in a corner of her heart. Delta knew he preferred to work late most nights, and the fact that he was coming home to share pizza with her after shift meant something. She wasn't sure what yet, but it did.

Who says I haven't already eaten?

D

Delta smiled as she hit the sent button, and within seconds her phone buzzed again.

Doesn't matter, you're always hungry. You know, saving the world and all that.

N

Delta laughed and couldn't help but think that someday this innocent flirting and simmering attraction between them would lead her down a path of no return. She shoved the thought away and texted him back.

Now that you mention it, I did save a man today. I'll provide dessert.

D

As her phone confirmed the message was sent, Delta cringed inwardly. That message could be construed many ways, and she wasn't ready for the implications.

Can't wait.

N

Delta read Neal's message over numerous times but couldn't be sure how he interpreted her message. She would just have to wait and see for herself. The fact that she wondered about being intimate with Neal without having fear clutch at her heart was already a step in the right direction.

Chapter 15

NEAL LOOKED FORWARD to going home. Something that had never been the highlight of his day before now became the one thing he looked forward to everyday. He stepped into his apartment and smiled as the scent hit his nostrils. During the past few weeks, a scent distinct to Delta had gained purchase in his apartment. Something soft and floral with an undertone of soap, a smell that made his apartment feel more like home than it ever did before.

For the past few years, he had avoided relationships altogether and had been convinced his reserve was a result of his previous girlfriends cheating on him. Now that he was considering a relationship again, Neal realized the scars had healed long ago. He just hadn't been interested in anyone until now.

Until Delta.

His neighbor with the lithe body and frightened eyes intrigued and fascinated him in equal measures. Moving into the kitchen with the two pizza boxes, he noticed Delta comfortably draped over the couch, reading something on her phone.

"Pizza's here," Neal said, setting the boxes down.

Delta's head turned towards him, and a wide smile split her face in two as beautiful green eyes shined up at him. "So are you."

As soon as she said the words, Neal could see she regretted it.

He laughingly shook his head and took out some plates. "I got the one you like and a spicy chicken. Would you like to try the chicken?"

"Yes, please. I've been craving something spicy all week." Delta walked into the kitchen barefoot with her jeans riding low on her hips and an oversized white jersey hanging off one shoulder. Neal almost drooled at the sight; she looked sexy as hell.

"Wine?" she asked, laughing at his mouth all but hanging open.

"Yes, thanks."

"Great, 'cause I feel like a glass or two tonight."

"Good day at work?" Neal asked as he plated the slices of pizza.

"No, and yes," Delta said, placing a glass of red wine in front of him before hitching herself onto the counter.

"Would you like to tell me about it?" He could tell she looked happy, so whatever hadn't been good wasn't that bad.

"Well, my day started out with the arson investigator paying me a visit."

"I'm sure that's standard procedure?" Neal asked, biting into the spicy chicken slice. The roof of his mouth exploded, even as the delicious taste tingled his taste buds. It was like being in a war zone and eating your favorite chocolate ice cream. Something about the contrast made you appreciate the taste and balance even more.

"Yes, it is." Delta narrowed her eyes at Neal. "Are you all right? You're sweating like a pig. Are you ill?"

Neal swallowed the tears and blinked a few times before wiping his brow with his sleeve. "I'm fine, so's the spicy chicken."

Delta threw her head back and laughed. "You really need to eat more spicy food! Anyway, so yes it's normal for the arson investigator to pay the victim a visit, but it's not normal for her to insinuate that I'm a pyro firebug and an attention seeker."

"Oh boy, what happened?" Neal asked, grabbing a bottle of water from the fridge to put out the inferno raging in his mouth.

"I told her if it were me, I would've been more inventive," Delta said, biting into the spicy chicken pizza as if it were strawberries and ice cream.

"Do you want some water?" Neal asked, moving towards the fridge.

Delta swallowed and shrugged. "Is this the blazing inferno pizza? Seriously, Neal, you have the taste buds of a two-year-old." She took another bite, relishing it.

"So you told her you would've been more inventive? I'm sure she took it well."

"Actually, she didn't have a choice. We got called out."

Neal still had trouble imagining Delta being called out to dangerous situations every day, but the fact that she made it home after every shift had increased his respect for her profession. "Fire?"

"No, suicide attempt."

"Why would you be called out?" Almost every time Delta came off shift Neal learned something. Most people thought firefighters only put out fires, but it had become evident to Neal that the job encompassed everything from dousing fires to cutting victims out of wrangled cars, and now suicide attempts.

"Sometimes when someone is trying to commit suicide and it's either in the public eye or a high building or really when no one else is available to talk them down, we're called."

"Did he do it?" Neal asked carefully.

Delta smiled broadly and shook her head. "No, I talked him down."

"You? Wait...what?"

"Remember that house fire last week, where the woman was killed?" When Neal nodded, Delta continued. "It was the husband. He had just buried his wife and unborn baby this morning and didn't have a will to live anymore. We found him on the wrong side of the guardrail, ready to leap."

"And you talked him down?"

"Yes."

"Wow. Congratulations, Delta, you really saved that man's life." Neal clinked his glass against hers.

"I know, so it's a good day. How was yours?"

"Remember my case last week? The abused woman?"

"Yes. He was found guilty, right?" Delta asked, picking up another slice of pizza.

"Yes. The sentencing was carried out this morning. He got

about ten years, but he'll only serve seven on good behavior."

"So is that a good sentence or bad?" Delta asked, tilting her head. She rarely asked Neal about his cases.

"I was hoping for longer, but it was unrealistic given the evidence. It's good in the sense that he'll have a record. Even if he gets out, it will follow him, and when he does get out, I'll make sure there is a restraining order in place for the wife."

"I'm happy you're happy," Delta said, wiping some cheese from her chin.

"I like having you here," Neal thought to himself. When he noticed Delta's eyes widening, he realized he had said it aloud. "I didn't mean to scare you. It's just I've never wanted to live with someone, but I'm actually enjoying having you here."

"Well, I do try to rinse the sink most mornings and try not to shed on your couch," Delta said before leaning forward and using her thumb to wipe some spicy sauce from his chin.

Neal felt his arousal stir at her soft touch and reached for her hand; he slowly brought it to his mouth and sucked the sauce off her thumb. Delta softly gasped at the intimacy, but she didn't pull her hand back. Her eyes had turned the color of the ocean right before a storm. Instead of fear, Neal recognized invitation.

He slowly stepped between Delta's knees, her hand still in his, and kissed her knuckles while keeping his eyes on hers, waiting for her to retreat.

When she didn't, Neal leaned in and softly brushed his lips against her forehead. Her hair smelled like a cloud of coconuts and exotic fruit. A soft sigh escaped her mouth as she lifted her chin to offer him her mouth. Carefully, Neal brushed his thumb over her soft pink lips while his own tongue glided over his own lips.

Fraction by fraction, he leaned in until his lips were softly caressing hers. Delta's hands moved around his body and gripped his back, inching him even closer. With his control balancing a tight rope, Neal kissed her, this time with meaning. Delta tilted her head and opened her mouth, giving him access. Tasting of spice and mystery, her tongue dueled with his.

His hands slid up the sides of her face and into her hair. As he pulled her closer, he could feel his own heart beating against the walls of his chest. Neal had never taken such care with a woman before and didn't want his control to snap and frighten Delta away forever.

He felt her melt against him as his one hand trailed to the back of her neck and over her shoulder, then slipped around to the side of her breast. He softly grazed it with his thumb and earned another soft gasp from Delta. Her fingers had started cruising up and down the muscled ridges of his back, and Neal had to stop himself from slipping his hands under her hips and carrying her to his bed.

Instead his hand inched around, cupping her breast before his thumb found the hard nub underneath. He rubbed over it, and in an instant, the kiss turned from sweet to hungry. They nipped and teased each other's mouths, finding it more gratifying than the wine and the pizza. This hunger had been lingering since they first met. Neal wanted more; he wanted to taste her, to explore her body. Giving into the urge, he trailed his mouth down the side of her neck, over her smooth ivory skin. His lips followed the contour of her neck where the sweater had slid over her shoulder, and he was happily surprised to find no bra. He pressed a kiss against her bare skin before slowly tugging the sweater down to reveal her breast. She was beautiful.

Neal had found her swollen nub and was closing his mouth over it when Delta jerked back. Neal held his hands up in the air. "What?"

"What the hell do you think you're doing?" Delta's voice was low and filled with accusation.

"Excuse me?" Neal asked, his control slipping. "You were right there with me; don't act like this was all me."

"You're taking advantage of the fact that I'm living here," Delta said without looking him in the eye and hopped off the counter. Standing barefoot in front of him with her eyes wide and frightened, she was a few inches shorter than Neal. "I told you I don't want this."

Neal's control snapped. As Delta turned to run to her room, Neal grabbed her wrist and flung her around. "I have never and will never take advantage of a woman. You were giving me a clear signal; I didn't misinterpret or take advantage. You're the one that doesn't know what you want, although it's clear you want me as much as I want you."

"I don't," Delta said jutting out her chin defiantly.

"Bullshit! I can tell from the way you touched me, the way you smile when I walk through the door; you want this just as much as I do." Neal let go of her wrist and took two steps back with his hands in the air in a gesture of surrender. "So I'll tell you this. I won't touch you again, Delta, not if your eyes are begging me to, or if the moment is right. The next time you want me to touch you, you'll come to me. But I'm done guessing whether you're going to blow hot or cold each time I do."

Neal grabbed his keys and his phone and walked out of his apartment, leaving Delta staring after him in confusion after the door slammed on his way out.

As the chilly evening air hit him on the sidewalk and clarity prevailed, Neal knew he shouldn't have taken things so far, but if she wasn't going to tell him what was going on inside her head, how was he ever going to know?

Chapter 16

DELTA FLINCHED AS the door slammed behind Neal. She didn't like it, but she had to admit she was wrong. She had wanted Neal to kiss her, to touch her, to glide his hands over her skin with care. Then what went wrong?

She asked herself the question countless times but couldn't pin it down. After setting the kitchen back to rights and rinsing their wine glasses, she searched for Nadine's number on her phone. At their last meeting, Nadine had insisted Delta take her number and let her know when she had an evening free for a girls' night. Without hesitation, she dialed Nadine's number.

"Hiya," came the smooth, throaty voice over the phone.

"Hi, Nadine. It's Delta."

"Girl, I've been waiting for you to call." Delta could hear Nadine smiling over the phone.

"I know, and I'm sorry I haven't called you yet. I'd love to have a ladies night, but right now I need advice."

"Shoot," Nadine said, sounding all business. "That SOB isn't back, is he?"

Delta laughed. "No, he isn't. It's about Neal."

"Ooh, the roommate. I'm all ears."

Delta glanced at her watch and saw it was just shy of nine o'clock. "Actually, if you're not busy I can meet you somewhere; just tell me where."

"Fine, meet me at that new Irish pub downtown. I'll be there in ten minutes."

"Great. Thanks, Nadine. I'm buying." Delta ended the call, grabbed a jacket, and hoped Nadine would have the advice she needed.

The pub was bustling with activity. Delta could spot the regulars as she moved past the bar; they sat facing forward, chatting with one another and calling the barman by his first name. In a shady corner, there were two men sitting with eyes darting towards the door. *Probably a shady deal,* Delta thought as her eyes scanned the pub for Nadine.

"Over here," Nadine called from across the pub. She had gotten them a booth which already boasted two glasses of wine. "I hope you don't mind that I ordered wine; you didn't seem like a bourbon type of girl."

Delta laughed, happy that she had called Nadine. Her careless banter and honesty was exactly what Delta needed. "Thanks, but I'm still buying."

"Next round. So what's up?" Nadine asked, bracing her elbows on the table.

Delta sighed and shook her head. "It's like I'm lost in a maze and just when I think I've found the exit, someone moves a wall."

"Honey, our whole lives are a maze. You just need to start running faster."

"I know, but urghhh! Enough with the figurative speech. I want Neal, but I freeze when he touches me."

Nadine laughed long and hard before finally putting her hand over Delta's. "Why didn't you just say that? So let me get this straight: you want to get jiggy, but your brain is acting like a cock-block?"

Delta nearly spat her wine over table and quickly glanced

around to check if someone had heard Nadine. "Shhh," Delta urged. "That's basically the problem."

"Right, so we need to figure out how to get your brain to start cooperating with your hormones."

"Not an easy fix, I suppose. This was stupid, Nadine. I'm sorry for bringing you out here for something stupid." Delta was pushing back from the table when Nadine's hand closed over hers.

When she spoke, her voice was caring and empathetic. "Honey, it's not stupid. It feels stupid because you've never been here before, and you need to reprogram your brain. It isn't an easy fix, but there's more than one way to skin a cat."

Delta smiled sadly. "Does the cat get skinned in the end?"

"Sometimes quicker than other times, but yes, it does get skinned. So let's start with what Neal knows about you."

Delta swallowed and looked straight into Nadine's chocolate brown eyes. "He knows I'm a firefighter and that I recently moved to Wilmington."

"Does he know about your ex?"

"No."

"Then we start with that."

About two hours and another glass of wine later, Delta let herself into the apartment. The lights were switched off, but Delta noticed Neal's keys on the kitchen island. He came home.

Nadine had given her good advice, complete with an execution plan, but Delta couldn't wait until tomorrow evening. She needed to execute it now, while she felt courageous.

She quickly went to the bathroom to check her hair and makeup and splashed on some perfume before kicking off her shoes.

Delta tiptoed towards Neal's room barefoot and hesitated before she turned the door knob. Taking a deep breath, she thought of what it felt like when he kissed her earlier. It didn't feel threatening, it felt...magical. Yes, it was a cliché, she thought, but it was the first time she felt that way.

She quietly turned the knob and tiptoed into his room. Neal's figure was turned away from her under the bedspread, and the nightlight cast an ethereal glow through the room. Feeling courageous and naughty, she moved to the other side of the bed and softly climbed on.

Neal moaned in his sleep before turning towards her.

"I'd like to talk to you," Delta whispered, leaning towards

him.

Neal grunted, and for a moment, Delta felt foolish for sneaking into his room late at night. She was swaying her body to get up when she felt Neal's hand close over her wrist.

"I'm listening."

Delta turned back to him. He didn't open his eyes but softly started circling his thumb over her wrist. Knowing he was listening but not looking at her, Delta was grateful and started to talk.

"I met Craig Swift just over three years ago. It was just after my mother died, and I was in a bad place. Craig noticed me and made me feel special. After joining a support group for abused women, I now know most abusers do that at first to gain loyalty. For two years, he was the perfect boyfriend: considerate, kind, and charming. Oh God, he was charming." She put her hands over her eyes at the memory. "All my friends were jealous because I had such a charismatic boyfriend." Delta swallowed the tears that threatened to fall.

"I'm listening," Neal said soothingly.

"The first time he hit me it was because I nagged him after a long day at the office. You see, Craig was a corporate lawyer. He's at one of the top firms in Chicago, and the pressure that comes with it...you understand? I told myself it was my fault for nagging him and that I should respect the work he did. The following day, he brought me chocolates and flowers and apologized profusely, promising it wouldn't happen again. The second time he hit me, I knew I had to do something. After he left for work the next morning, I headed straight to the police. They took the photos and the statement and told me they would take care of it. I played the part of the perfect girlfriend for two weeks, waiting for the police to come knocking or for something to happen. When it didn't, I headed back to the precinct. With barely a glance, the guy that handled my case told me my paperwork had been lost. You see, I knew he was lying because he didn't even open a file or look at his computer. He looked me straight in the eye and told me everything was lost."

Neal cursed and sat up, taking both Delta's hands in his. "That's why you hate lawyers? Sorry for interrupting; please go on," Neal said before shaking his head.

She inhaled deeply and continued her story. "I knew then that he had the paperwork destroyed or misplaced or whatever you want to call it. That's when I knew I needed to get out. I had started saving for our wedding a year before and began pushing any funds I could into that account, hoping Craig wouldn't find out. I nearly had enough; I was planning to leave within the next month when he came home drunk one evening. I don't even know what the fight was about. I remember me asking how his day was, and the next second I felt my eye socket explode with pain as his fist landed. I tried to fight back, but he was stronger. After a few punches, the last one had me falling on the floor. He stood over me with whiskey on his breath and told me I was useless before kicking me. That's when he broke my ribs. I remember counting four major injuries. The bump on my head from falling against the side table, my swollen eye, the cut on my lip, and my ribs. By the time I came to, he was passed out on the couch. I crawled to the bedroom, packed a duffel bag, and made it to the bus station. I got on the first bus and didn't get off until I reached Wilmington."

When Neal didn't say anything, Delta felt her throat close. It was too much, too much to lay on someone you've only known for a few weeks. "Neal?"

"I knew."

"What?" Delta all but jumped back on the bed. "You did a check or something on me?" The feeling of betrayal had Delta narrowing her eyes at Neal.

"I didn't have to. The first time I touched you, I noticed the look in your eyes. It's a look I'm sorry to say I've seen too many times in my line of work."

"You knew?" Delta asked, settling again. "Why didn't you say anything?"

"It wasn't my place; I knew sooner or later you would tell me if you felt the same way I did."

Delta smiled wryly. "So now you know how I feel?"

"No, now I know you know what you want, and whatever that is, I'm a part of it."

Delta leaned closer, her mouth inches from his. "Right now, I'd like you to kiss me again."

"I will, but first tell me if he knows where you are?"

"No, and I don't intend to let him know."

Neal nodded and slowly brushed his lips over hers. Delta sighed at the touch. Neal's arms enfolded her as his mouth caressed hers; soft moans and gasps escaped her as his fingers trailed over her back and his tongue enticed hers.

She could taste his hunger for her; it reciprocated her own. When Neal's hand slipped below her sweater to caress her sides, Delta felt the fear slowly clutch her chest.

She couldn't help it when her back stiffened. Neal pulled back. "Thank you for telling me."

Delta blinked twice and realized Neal was giving her an escape. It took all her courage, but she got off the bed and walked around to his side. She climbed into his lap and hooked her arms around his neck before looking deep into his sky-blue eyes. "Neal, this is me asking you not to stop. Make love to me..." She searched his eyes for the right words. "Just be patient with me."

"Delta? If you're not ready, we don't have to," Neal said, taking her head in his hands.

"I'm ready. I want to be with you."

Neal kissed her again, both more passionate and more demanding. Delta answered the demand eagerly. Her heart pounded in her chest from excitement, not fear, as she dragged her fingers through his short hair. This time when his hands slipped beneath her sweater, Delta gasped from delight, not panic, and threw back her head, absorbing the feel of Neal's fingers against her back.

Warm, hot kisses were trailed along the slope of her neck until Neal scraped his teeth over her bare shoulder.

Need flooded Delta's system. Hot and seductive, it flowed

through her veins, wanting more of the drug that Neal was to her system.

Even in the beginning, it was never like this with Craig, Delta thought as Neal's lips cruised lower, pushing the sweater down over her breasts. She hadn't bothered with a bra, a luxury from having small breasts, and was now grateful she hadn't. As Neal's hands grasped her bottom, his mouth closed over her breast. The moist warmth of his mouth had Delta gasping; as soon as she did, she was afraid Neal would stop. "Don't stop."

She felt Neal's laugh against her breast. "I don't plan to."

Delta closed her eyes and enjoyed the feeling of a man's hands on her body in pursuit of pleasure and not pain.

Chapter 17

NEAL LOVED HER taste, her responsiveness. He had known that when he finally had Delta to himself, it would be special, but he never imagined the way he would feel.

Even as his blood heated with arousal, his fists itched to get hold of the bastard that had hurt her. The wheels in his mind were already spinning; first thing in the morning, he would find out where Craig Swift currently was. He would try to find out who had been paid off to lose Delta's paperwork, and he would...

All coherent thoughts left his mind as Delta's nails scraped along his back. The time for thinking had past; the time for exploring had just begun.

Their hands explored as their mouths tasted. Clothes were discarded carelessly, but care was taken with touch. Delta's fingers moved tentatively over his bare torso. As she explored his body,

Neal had to control his need to take her immediately.

This was a big step for her, and he needed to make sure she had time to adjust mentally and physically for what was to come. He wanted tonight to be one of the best nights of her life, and for that he would need patience and control.

As she reached his manhood, she closed her hand around him, and Neal gasped at her soft touch.

"Did I do something wrong?" Delta asked him with wide eyes.

"No, that's just it. You're doing everything right." Neal smiled at her as she explored a little more.

Finally, Neal couldn't take it anymore. He slowly pulled her up and handed her the protection he had gotten from the bedside drawer. He clenched his teeth as she slowly rolled it onto him. Once he was fully sheathed, Neal took her hips and lifted her, nudging her entrance. He rested his hands on her thighs, giving her total control.

Delta leisurely sank down on him, and Neal watched her eyes turn cloudy with arousal. She started rocking him back and forth, her hair bouncing on her shoulders.

Neal needed to do something; he needed to touch her, taste her, anything but lie still and watch her. If he didn't do something, he was going to lose control.

He cupped her breasts and slowly circled her nipples with his thumb until he felt her body start to clench around him. Knowing she was close, Neal slipped a hand between them and found the bundle of nerves nestled in her folds.

Expertly, he flicked it until Delta started moving faster. Neal felt the wave climbing and climbing until Delta clenched around him in ecstasy. Grabbing her hips, he met her thrust and rode the wave until they were both washed out on the other side, sated and breathless.

Delta collapsed onto his chest with a giggle. "That was…"

"Amazing," Neal said breathlessly.

She pushed herself up and looked into his eyes. The frightened look was gone; instead, a lazy afterglow shone in them. "Thank you."

"Same goes." Neal smiled up at her as he brushed a stray strand of hair away from her eyes.

"I didn't think I would ever be able to…" Neal could hear the emotion in her voice.

"But you did. Thank you for telling me and for trusting me."

"I wanted to do it after my next shift. Cook you a nice dinner, dress pretty, and seduce you…" Delta rested her head on his chest, and Neal lazily tickled her back as she spoke again.

"I've been thoroughly seduced. No need for dinner and pretty dresses."

Delta laughed before her expression turned serious. "I don't want to mislead you, Neal; I'm not looking for a relationship."

Neal thought of the times he had said that himself and realized it wasn't nice being on the receiving end. He knew it didn't matter what he said now; it had to be Delta's choice. He decided to lighten the mood a little instead. "So you just want to use me?"

Delta's laugh sounded through the room, careless and happy. "Not exactly... Well maybe a little. Can't we just be…friends?"

It was Neal's turn to laugh. "With benefits?"

"Exactly."

"I really like being your friend right now," Neal said as he felt himself harden again. He nudged her entrance, and Delta giggled.

"Already?"

"I've been waiting two months to do this. I've got a lot of pent-up energy stored for my new best friend."

Delta flipped off him onto her back. "Well come on then, show me how much."

Neal read the invitation in her eyes and didn't need a second invitation.

"Well, I'll be! If it isn't the prodigal son returning," Susan Sullivan said as Neal walked through the back door. She stood in front of the stove wearing bright orange Crocs and a matching apron over faded jeans. Her greying blonde hair framed her face in a melody of tight curls.

"Hi, Mom, and really, it isn't that bad," Neal said, grabbing a beer from the fridge, knowing she wasn't completely wrong. Before Delta, he would drop by his parents' house at least once a week, and he had barely been by since Delta had moved in.

"Not that bad? We've hardly seen you in two months! We haven't even seen you since the fire at your apartment."

"You've seen me," Neal said, frowning and feeling guilty.

"Ha!" Susan said, slipping a pasta dish into the oven. "Are you staying for dinner? Max and Lisa will be here."

"I can't, Mom. I can't stay long. I need to be home by dinner." Neal stood up as his father joined them in the kitchen. Mackenzie Sullivan walked into the kitchen and playfully smacked his wife's bum, earning him a slap with the dishcloth, before he walked to Neal. His t-shirt was a faded blue, and his khaki pants were frayed at the pockets. Neal smiled as his father's faded green eyes smiled at him. Mackenzie Sullivan pulled Neal into a bear hug before standing back and giving him an assessing glance. His father's broad shoulders and fierce stare reminded Neal that his father was once an important businessman, a top designer at one of the best architectural firms in Wilmington.

"How are you?" Mac asked, holding Neal's face in his hands.

"Mac, tell him to stay for dinner."

"I'm fine, Dad, and I just told mom I can't stay for dinner," Neal said pleadingly to Mac. Once his mom decided on something, it wasn't easy to get out of it.

Mac frowned at Neal before winking mischievously. "Has it got something to do with the sexy firefighter staying with you?"

"What? You have a firefighter living with you?" Susan slipped the apron over her head and joined Mac and Neal with a questioning glance.

"Let me guess: Caleb?" Neal asked.

"Doesn't matter who told me; the strange thing is that you didn't." Mac's eyebrows raised slightly.

"Enough!" Susan said, huffing. "What's going on?"

Mac turned to Susan. "Suze, remember when Neal was stuck in the elevator? The firefighter that saved him was a woman; it just so happens that she's his neighbour. The apartment that burned down was hers, and Neal offered her a place to stay."

Susan narrowed her eyes and turned to Neal for verification. "It's true, Mom."

She clapped her hands together and kissed Neal hard on the mouth. "I'm so glad, honey! When can we meet her?"

"Mom, slow down! We're not..." Neal paused. How did he explain this to his mom? "Friends with benefits" wasn't exactly a term you shared with your parents.

"Oh please, that pause right there just told me you are something. So when are you bringing her for dinner? Tomorrow night could work."

"Uh." Neal tried to think a way out of this one but struggled. "Mom, it's complicated."

"How?" Susan asked, with her hands on her hips.

"She..."

"Oh for goodness sake, Neal, just spit it out," Mac said impatiently.

"Delta was…"

Susan beamed at Mac. "Oh, Mac, her name is Delta. What a pretty name."

"Suze, let the boy speak," Mac said before turning back to Neal.

"Mom, Delta was abused by her previous boyfriend, and we're not officially seeing each other. We're more like friends, good friends."

Susan's hand clutched her throat. "The poor girl! Neal, is she all right?"

"She's fine now, but she's still easily spooked, especially by strange men."

"See, I told you the children think I'm strange," Mac said, shaking his head.

Susan laughed at her husband before turning back to Neal. "I promise I'll keep your dad on a leash and duct tape Max's mouth."

"I'll ask her," Neal conceded, knowing he wasn't going to win.

"Great! While you figure out exactly what she means to you, I'd like to get to know her a little better. Shame, you live so close and we don't even know what's going on in your life," Susan said turning to the fridge to take out the makings for the salad.

Mac stepped closer to Neal and whispered. "Do you know who he is?"

Neal nodded.

"Then I suppose you've got someone keeping an eye on him." Neal recognized his father's protectiveness, even though he had yet to meet Delta.

"Taken care of," Neal said, knowing his father would understand.

The morning after he had made love to Delta, he had gotten a private investigator to look into Craig Swift. There were sealed records from when he was a teenager than Neal couldn't look into, but what he did find was disturbing. Craig was known to be aggressive and was currently being looked at for money laundering and bribing police officers. The picture he had received from the private investigator wasn't pretty and not one he thought Delta knew wholly about.

She had gone on shift last night and was due home any minute now. Besides the fact that Neal couldn't wait to see her, he didn't want her to be at home alone. He had a nasty feeling about the arson in Delta's apartment and this Swift guy. He hadn't mentioned it to her, but it was enough for him to keep an extra eye out for her.

"Do you know what food she likes?" Susan asked, setting down a cutting board, a cucumber, a pineapple, and a couple of peppers.

Neal laughed. "Anything."

"Nonsense, girls are always fussy. Just look at Lisa, she hates cheese. Who hates cheese?" Susan said, throwing her hands in the air.

"Mom, believe me. Delta eats anything and isn't afraid of a second helping."

Mac laughed. "Sounds like a girl after my own heart."

Susan thought for a moment before frowning. "If she's a firefighter, she must need all the energy she can get. Maybe we should carbo-load? Isn't that what they call it?"

Neal smiled. His mom always went out of her way for anyone. "Yes, Mom that's what it called. But really, Delta will eat anything, even if it burns a hole in your throat."

Mac turned to Susan. "Maybe you could make chili dogs?"

"Mac, its times like this that I know why I married you! What a great idea; it wouldn't be too formal, and we can eat out back. Chili dogs it is," Susan said, taking Neal's hands in her own.

"Don't worry, honey, we'll be careful with her. I can see she's important."

He just hoped his mother didn't try a new chili recipe. The one she had already had him sweating just thinking about it.

Susan squeezed his hand and stage-whispered into Neal's ear, "Don't worry. I'll make you your own not-so-hot chili."

Mac's laughter boomed through the room.

"Thanks, Mom," Neal said, shaking his head even though he was grateful to know he would be going home with his taste buds in tact.

And that was it, Neal thought as he drove home. His parents didn't need to know more than that he cared for Delta. They would accept her regardless of her past or the danger that followed her. Now he just needed to do one thing: he needed to invite Delta to dinner with the Sullivans.

Chapter 18

"WHAT? NO, YOU must be crazy! We've just become...whatever...and you already want me to meet your parents?" Delta shook her head, completely caught off guard by Neal's invitation.

She had been looking forward to coming home to him the whole day, and now she just wanted to escape.

"Delta, it's not that kind of dinner. My parents want to thank you for saving my life. And before you say it wasn't in danger, you weren't the one in the elevator. And, besides, you like eating, so why not enjoy a home-cooked meal with my family?" Neal was either trying to keep his mother happy, or he was paranoid about leaving her alone at home. Delta wasn't sure which scale was heavier, but she had a feeling both were in play.

"Neal, I'm not going to dinner at your parents', and that's

final." Delta laughed and walked towards her bedroom. After tossing her jacket on the bed and slipping into her flip flops, she headed back to the kitchen where Neal was stirring a pot.

"Have you heard anything on the investigation?" Neal asked.

"No," Delta said, grabbing a bottle of water from the fridge. "It was arson. But since there were no prints and no one saw anything, that's about that. There's not much more they can do."

"Shit, Delta. Even more reason for you not to stay home alone. Please just come to dinner tomorrow night? I don't want to spend the whole evening wondering if my place is being burned to the ground."

Horror struck Delta like lightning. Neal also thought she lit up her apartment. "What? Oh, you're kidding." She quickly recovered when she saw Neal smiling over his shoulder at her. More and more, she was getting to know this side of him. He had a mysterious way with words, and Delta was still learning when he was kidding and when he was serious. But when he smiled at her like that, butterflies flitted in her tummy, and all thoughts escaped her mind.

"My parents would really like it if you would come, and if you don't come, my mother is going to hound me until you do."

"Neal...I really don't think it's a good idea. What if they don't like me? What if I freak out when your father or your brothers touch me?" Delta chewed her thumbnail, a habit she broke about ten years ago, but Neal's insistence made her as nervous as a teenager before her first date.

"You know, it's fine. If you don't want to go, you don't have to. I'll have a cop on the door while I'm out, and I'll try and bring you back a chili dog." His back was turned to her, but Delta could hear the smile in his voice. Her mouth watered at the thought of a home-cooked chili-dog. "Did you just say chili dog?" Delta asked, slipping her hands around his waist as she leaned her head on his shoulder, ignoring the comment about the cop. She wasn't going to let fear dictate how she lived her life ever again.

"I did, but it's fine. I'll just tell my mom you don't want to meet them."

"You're playing dirty, Neal," Delta whispered against his neck before kissing him. He smelled of forests and soap, a combination that had become an addiction for Delta.

"No, I'm not. I'm simply stating it like it is," Neal said as he continued stirring.

"Does your mother have your two-year-old taste buds, or does she make a decent chili dog?" Delta said thoughtfully.

"I normally pass on the chili; she makes me my own little bowl of tepid chili," Neal said proudly.

Delta laughed and struggled to imagine strong and powerful Neal being coddled by his mother; maybe it would be interesting to see the interaction between him and his parents. "I'll go tomorrow night, on one condition."

"Anything," Neal said, turning and putting his arms around her.

"If I say the code word, you get me out of there." Delta knew she sounded pathetic, but she didn't want to have a panic attack in the middle of a Sullivan family dinner.

"Deal. What's the codeword?" Neal asked with his mouth an inch away from Delta's.

"Chili," Delta said before pressing her lips against his and her body flush against his firm torso. The thought of chili disappeared as Neal's hands started cruising over her body, heating her blood with every touch.

When Neal pulled up next to a blue Victorian house with white trim late afternoon the following day, Delta felt her palms grow sweaty. She had never been afraid of meeting strangers, but somehow, today was important. She and Neal hadn't put a label on their relationship, and yet it felt like she was meeting her boyfriend's parents, which she actually was.

She got out and walked onto the wraparound porch, glancing at the porch swing. It was weathered, but Delta could imagine many nights had been spent on that swing discussing problems, falling in love, and even consoling one another in times of need. Jasmine climbed the corner pillar of the porch, releasing its rich fragrance on the balmy evening. One day, Delta wanted a house with a large porch and a porch swing to be able to do all of that with the man she loved. She felt Neal's hand close around her smaller hand before he opened the door.

"We're here," Neal called out as he stepped into the cozy living room. The walls were decorated with family pictures ranging from first birthdays to wedding photos. The house smelt of potpourri and clean linen, and Delta felt instantly welcomed. A woman in her early twenties walked into the room wearing a spaghetti strap top and long billowing bright skirt. Dark glossy locks tumbled over her shoulders, even as her sky-blue eyes smiled at Delta. "Hi, I'm Lisa, and you must be my brother's hero."

For a moment, Delta felt inadequate next to the beautiful woman standing in front of her, but as Lisa's hand rested on Delta's shoulder, part of the nerves disappeared. "Barely his hero, but for the time being, his roommate."

Lisa smiled and twirled the long strand of beads hanging around her neck through her fingers as a look passed between her and Neal.

"Mom and Dad are waiting out back," Lisa said before turning and leaving her and Neal alone.

"Your sister is beautiful," Delta said as soon as they were alone.

Neal laughed. "Thanks, she'd love that, although her looks are the cause of many heartbreaks in Wilmington."

"Why?" Delta asked as Neal led her through the dining room into the kitchen.

"Because Lisa is an incurable romantic, she falls in love at least three times a month. The problem is she soon realizes it isn't love, and by the time she does, the poor guy's already fallen for her." Neal shrugged.

Delta nodded and noticed a bright green patch of grass just beyond the kitchen window. The grass was surrounded by bright spring garden beds, and a large oak tree stood in the center. There was an old man standing by a grill who Delta guessed to be Neal's dad. A small woman with curly blonde hair, wearing a tie-dye shirt, was decorating the outdoor table with snippets of flowers.

"Come on, time for you to meet them," Neal said, noticing her watching his parents. Delta followed him outside, where both his parents put down everything and joined them just beyond the backdoor.

"You must be Delta," the woman said, smiling at Delta. Delta held her breath when Neal's father moved closer.

"This is Susan, and I'm Mac. We're this brat's parents." Mac smiled before pointing at Neal, and everyone laughed. Delta glanced between them and noticed the easy affection between Neal and his parents. "Welcome to our home." Mac didn't move to shake hands or to hug her, and Delta released her breath, feeling relieved.

"Thank you for inviting me," Delta said smiling at both Mac and Susan. Delta could see that Neal was a younger version of Mac but had his mother's blue eyes. Lisa joined them and playfully punched Neal in the arm. "I hear Mom made you special baby chili?"

Neal frowned and turned to his mom. "Really, you had to tell everyone?"

Susan shrugged before smiling at Delta. "Poor Neal is the only one in the family that can't handle a little chili, so his siblings tease him endlessly for it. Why don't you quickly help me bring out the rolls while the guys start up the grill?" She turned to Lisa, and Delta noticed a white peace symbol from the seventies on the back of her bright tie-dye shirt. "Lisa, you can make sure everyone's got a drink."

Delta laughed and followed Susan into the kitchen. "I really appreciate you coming by today," Susan said as she picked up a square plastic container filled to the brim with hotdog rolls before handing the napkins to Delta.

"To be honest, I didn't think I was going to. I barely know Neal," Delta said as she accepted the napkins Susan handed to her.

"You might not know him yet, but I do, and let me tell you, I haven't seen him smile in long time like he does since he got stuck in a certain elevator."

Delta laughed. "Really, everyone keeps going back to the elevator. It's my job."

"Yes, it might be. But making my son happy isn't, and you're doing that as well." Susan winked mischievously and left the kitchen before Delta could answer with a witty rebuttal.

Standing in the kitchen holding onto paper napkins, Delta watched Susan whisper something to Mac and the smile they shared. Neal was talking to his sister as he pulled a beer out of a tub of ice. From where she was standing, they truly looked like the perfect family.

"They don't bite," a voice said from behind her. Delta got such a big fright that all the napkins went flying into the air and slowly drifted to the ground.

She was flinging around with her hand fisted, ready to defend, when two strong hands rested on her shoulders. Light blonde hair with sun-lightened streaks hung loosely around a definitive masculine face. Perfectly straight white teeth were revealed as his smile spread.

"Relax, I'm Neal's brother Max. I didn't mean to scare you." His voice was easygoing, and even though Delta still felt scared, she knew he wasn't going to hurt her.

"It's all right, you just startled me," Delta said, catching her breath as she bent to pick up the napkins.

"I promise you I won't do it again. Next time, you might land a blow." He laughed again and helped Delta pick up the napkins. By the time she and Max joined everyone outside, her breathing had returned to normal, and once Neal put his arm around her shoulders and pulled her against him, her world righted itself again.

Mac was flipping sausages on the grill, sipping from a beer, and Susan and Lisa were discussing the garden, when Max offered her a beer.

"Sorry, I forgot to ask my parents to get some wine for you," Neal said considerately.

Delta smiled. "I drink beer." She popped the cap herself and sipped from the cold bitter liquid.

"So how does a woman become a firefighter?" Max asked without pause. Susan and Mac both shouted at the same time, "Max!"

"What? I'm sure it's a reasonable introductory question." Max shrugged and winked at Delta.

She had a feeling Max was the naughty one in the family. She knew Neal had another brother, Caleb, but he wasn't here tonight.

"It's not really that interesting. My dad was a firefighter." Delta shrugged.

Max laughed. "My dad's an architect, and my mother a hippie. That didn't influence any of our careers."

"Ha!" Lisa huffed. "Speak for yourself. Just because I'm going to be a marine biologist doesn't mean I neglect my inner hippie."

Delta could tell Lisa wasn't joking. With Lisa on the one side and Susan on the other side, Delta could tell being a hippie wasn't about how you dressed. Both women exuded a carefree air, and she was certain that men found it irresistible.

"So what do you do?" Delta asked, meeting Max's dark blue eyes. Even though he had his mother's blonde hair, his eyes were a darker shade of blue.

"Me?" Max shrugged. "I spend my life riding the river."

Delta laughed. "Another hippie then?" She caught the affectionate smile that Neal gave her before he spoke. "Actually, Max and a friend have a river boating company called Cape River Dreams."

"Oh, I've seen them on the Cape Fear. That's your business?"

Delta asked, genuinely interested. She would never have thought Max to be a business owner. He seemed so carefree and surfer-like. Although that would explain the tan and sun-lightened hair.

"Not really a business, more like a hobby." Max smiled.

"It pays the bills and a little more into your 401, so it's a business." Mac said from the grill. "He's just afraid that if anyone mistakes him for a business man, it wouldn't fit with the surfer hair."

Everyone laughed at Mac's comment, and Delta started to understand the family dynamic. Susan was the head of the house, even though Delta doubted Mac thought so. Lisa was the carefree baby of the family, and Mac and Max were both jokers with a knack for business.

"So what does your other brother do?" Delta asked Neal.

"He's going to be a daddy," Susan said, clapping her hands together.

"Mom, that's not a career." Max joked before turning to Delta. She had always found men a few years her senior more attractive, like Neal, who was two years older than she. But Delta had a feeling that Max attracted woman like flies with his charming smile and laid-back attitude. "Caleb is a writer. Have you ever heard of CB Sullivan?"

Delta nodded. She had been busy reading his latest bestseller when her apartment burned down and hadn't gotten around to replacing it yet. "Yes, I have."

"There you go," Max said, holding up his beer.

Delta's eyes widened as she turned to Neal. "Your brother is CB Sullivan, and you never told me?"

Neal shrugged. "I don't exactly pick up dates with my brother's credentials."

"Good thing this isn't a date, then." Delta smiled back.

"Mac, I like her. She puts Neal in his place," Susan said as she squeezed Delta's hand.

Delta laughed. "So where does he live?"

"Privileged information," Mac joked from the grill.

"In Maine," Susan said, beaming with pride. "He actually went to Maine to write last year. That's where he met Sarah Rothman. Well, long story short, Sarah, a southern debutante, had run away from her own wedding, and while she was trying to find herself, she found Caleb."

"My mom's leaving out the part where Sarah was nearly killed and how they are now married with a baby on the way," Lisa said casually from where she was now sprawling on the grass.

"Oh, a baby? When's the baby due?" Delta asked. She had always wanted a baby, but after Craig, she had reconsidered. She didn't want a child growing up in an abusive home. Maybe with Neal...

"Four years," Max said, interrupting her thoughts.

"Four months, you idiot!" Lisa said, kicking Max's shin from her spot on the grass.

Delta laughed as the scent of the chili sauce floated through the air. Her mouth watered in anticipation as Neal's hand slid around her waist, and his mouth whispered against her ear, "Just say the word."

Delta smiled up at him and said into his eyes, loud enough for everyone to hear, "The chili smells amazing. I'm so glad I came."

Neal's brow furrowed as he watched her, knowing it was her code word. Delta smiled at him. She knew she was teasing him, using their code word while her words meant something different. She leaned closer and whispered into his ear, "Relax. Although I'm serious, the chilli does smell amazing."

Delta laughed as she joined Lisa on the grass, feeling relaxed with friends for the first time in a long time.

Chapter 19

AS HE PULLED out of his parent's driveway later that evening, Neal thought back to what his mother had just said to him in the kitchen.

"I like her," Susan had said as she stacked the dishes.

"I do, too."

"Then do yourself a favor and hang on to her. I haven't seen you this happy since you played football in high school."

Neal had laughed at his mother's words, but in retrospect, he couldn't help but acknowledge them. Had it been that long since he had laughed freely and spent an entire evening without thinking about the law?

"What's wrong?" Delta asked from beside him.

"Nothing, that's just it. Absolutely nothing is wrong. It's just not a feeling I'm used to."

Delta placed her hand on his thigh and leaned her head against his shoulder. "I like your family."

"Thanks. I've tried to trade them in, but no one would take them. So I guess I'm stuck with them."

Delta laughed. "Really, I swear my tummy is going to ache from all the laughing. Your dad and Max really are a laugh a minute."

"I know. That's why I always stop by after a hard day. My dad would let me talk it out before making me laugh and taking my mind off it."

"What's Caleb like?" Delta asked as her hand softly started squeezing his thigh.

"Oh boy, are you star struck?" Neal asked playfully as they neared their apartment building.

Delta lightly swatted his leg a few inches below where it would matter. "No, I'm just trying to place him in my head. Lisa and your mother are similar, and Max and your dad are. You're a lot like your dad but more serious."

"Caleb's Caleb." Neal shrugged. "Although now that you ask…when's he's not writing, he's a lot like my dad and Max, but when he's in the middle of a book, he's like me on a bad day. No, make that like a hundred times worse."

Delta frowned. "Really?"

"Yeah, I guess it goes with the stuff he writes. You can't exactly be happy when you're writing about rape, torture, and murder, can you?"

"No, I guess not."

"I must say that Sarah's helped a lot with that. She knows how to handle him when he's in the grizzly part of a book, and she knows how to draw him back to life."

"Well, I must say Max is sweet and funny, and your dad is awesome. But I somehow prefer a dark and mysterious prosecutor that has a great sense of humor, or should I say sarcasm."

Neal laughed but gasped when her little finger grazed between his legs. "Delta?"

"Yes, Neal?" She looked up at him with big emerald-green eyes, smiling innocently.

"If you don't want me to crash this car, you'd better move your hand."

Delta withdrew her hand and folded both her hands in her lap before smiling at him mischievously. "I think it's time we got you over your fear of elevators, Mr. Sullivan."

Neal felt a rush of desire bolt through his bloodstream at her suggestive tone. He kept to the speed limit but made sure they reach the apartment within record time.

As soon as the elevator doors closed, Delta's mouth was pressed firmly against his, her hand roaming over the ridges and planes of his back. It was the first time Delta had made the first move. Neal was on foreign ground, not knowing if he should reciprocate or let her take the lead. He decided to do a little reciprocating as his fingers threaded into her hair and he took the kiss deeper.

With her body pressed against his, Neal completely forgot they were in an elevator until the "ding" sounded and the doors opened.

"Best elevator ride of my life," Neal said, taking her hand as they walked to the apartment. Delta's apartment was open, and they could hear carpenters sawing and hammering from inside. Neal ignored them as he unlocked his door; he wasn't ready for Delta to move out yet.

As he turned to lock the door behind them, he felt Delta's hands circling his waist before her lips pressed hot kisses against his neck.

"You've sure got an appetite going tonight," Neal joked as he turned around in her arms. Her eyes were a darker shade of green, like a river after a storm, as she looked at him.

"The chili was great, but it got the juices flowing for another type of hunger," Delta said seductively as her hands played over his hips.

"I'd be glad to oblige." Neal groaned as Delta's lips pressed against the hollow of his neck. He wanted nothing more than to scoop her up and take her straight to his bed, but tonight was for her to take the lead. "Just tell me what to do."

"Touch me," Delta whispered as she pulled her shirt over her head and dropped it on the floor. "I want to feel your hands on my skin."

With her eyes begging him, Neal had no choice but to oblige. His hands circled her waist before reaching behind her for the snap of her bra. It dropped to the floor, joining her shirt, before Neal's hands cupped her breasts.

Delta threw back her head and moaned as Neal bent down and took a swollen peak into his mouth. He lightly tugged with his teeth, drawing a giggle from Delta.

"You're impossible," Neal said against her skin.

"Why? Because I can't get enough of you?" Delta asked as her hands unsnapped his jeans.

"No, because I feel the same. Every time you touch me, I need to focus on not losing control."

Delta laughed as she tugged his jeans over his hips, brushing kisses along his muscled thighs. "Then let me take control for a change."

Neal leaned back against the door and did just that. But with each exploratory touch or hot kiss against his sensitive skin, the fever built.

Her hands deftly removed his socks and shoes before she nuzzled her way back to his hips.

"Time to lose your pants," Neal teased as Delta's lips moved over his abdomen.

She stepped back from him, keeping vivid green eyes focused on his as she started undoing her pants. She slowly shimmied out of them, and Neal couldn't help but gasp. He had seen her naked before, but there was a difference when someone stripped for you as their eyes remained locked on yours.

He felt his breath back up as she hooked her thumbs into her white cotton boy panties and slowly inched them down. He had never seen a more beautiful sight in his life.

Delta reached for his hand and led him to her room, another sign of her taking control. They had always made love in his room before. She gently pushed him down on the bed and laughed. "Just so you know, I don't have a clue what I'm doing."

Neal smiled encouragingly. "You're doing great so far."

As her hands reached for his boxers, dragging them over his hips to reveal his length, Neal heard her soft gasp. He wanted to touch her before fear set in, but before he could, she smiled seductively at him and reached for protection from the bedside drawer.

Her hands were tentative as they slowly slid the protection on, but Neal could feel the need in her touch. It mirrored his own as she held onto his shoulder and she climbed onto him.

Delta slowly slid onto him, her eyes hazing over from the sensation. Her scent, her essence and her body surrounded him. Never in his life had Neal imagined that anything could feel so right. Neal had always been serious, career-focused, and driven; never had he thought he would enjoy giving someone else control. But watching Delta take control would make tonight a night he would always remember, the night he helped her heal wounds he hadn't inflicted.

Once he was settled deep inside her, Delta leaned forward and kissed him before whispering in his ear, "Hang on, I'm hoping for a wild ride."

Neal started to laugh, but the laugh soon vanished when her fevered touch hungrily ran over his body as she rode him with her head thrown back.

Chapter 20

"JUST THE WOMAN I'm looking for." Delta flinched at the male voice as a hand grabbed her arm.

She swung around; ready to defend herself and the new life she had built for herself, when she realized it was Barry Williston, the landlord. "Hi, Barry. What can I do for you?"

"Ask not what you can do for me but what I can do for you." Barry said, winking at her.

Delta laughed. "And what can you do for me?" She glanced at her watch; she had about five minutes for Barry before she was going to be late for her shift.

Barry held out a bundle of keys with a smile a mile wide spreading across his face. "Your keys, my lady."

Delta frowned at the keys before she caught on. "My keys? Really? You mean my apartment is ready for me to move back?"

A satisfied grin spread over Barry's face. "Ready as can be, with new paint, appliances, flooring, and even a brand new 42-inch television to apologize for the inconvenience."

Before Delta could stop herself, she had her arms around Barry in a bear hug. There was no fear, only impulsive joy as she hugged him. She stepped back, noticing Barry's face had turned a bright red. "Thank you so much."

"Well, I like to keep my tenants happy."

Delta laughed. "I need to go, or I'm going to be late for work, but thanks again."

"No problem, Miss Eckhart. Have a good day, and be safe. Your job is very dangerous, especially for a woman."

Delta smiled and walked away. If only she had a quarter for every time she heard that.

Her shift went by in a happy haze; there were no raging fires, only a cat that needed to be rescued from the proverbial tree. On her way home the following morning, she stopped by a little gift shop.

She wanted to leave Neal something to remember his generosity by. A bell jingled on the door as she entered the little shop, and the scent of incense immediately overwhelmed her.

"Hello, dearie. Let me know if you're looking for something specific."

Delta waved and smiled at the shopkeeper and started perusing everything from crafts to trinkets. She had no idea what to get Neal, but she knew it should be special. She picked up a small statue of a donkey and was letting her fingers glide over the perfectly sculpted hair when she noticed it.

On the bottom shelf there was an assortment of handcrafted pens. Delta put the donkey back on the shelf and let her eyes feast on the craftsmanship and detail that went into every pen. There was a specific one that instantly caught her eye.

The clip was crafted into an arrow of shiny stainless steel, and the rest of the pen was a swirl of Caribbean blue and green. It made Delta think of Neal's eyes when he was in the throes of passion. She selected it and paid for it, hoping Neal would like it as much as she did.

Once the pen was neatly wrapped at home, Delta placed it on the kitchen island with a small handwritten thank you note next to it and headed across the hall to explore her "new" old apartment.

Barry was right. Everything was new and shiny, from the

shiny brushed metal kettle right through to the beautiful new faucets. The whole apartment had been painted a light dove-grey with white trim. The effect was stylish yet welcoming.

Delta was like a child in a candy store, running her hands over everything, from the new kitchen island right down to the new hardwood flooring, when there was a knock at the door.

"It's open," Delta called out, knowing it would be Neal.

"Really Delta, you shouldn't leave the door open," Neal scolded as he walked into the apartment. "Wow, I must say Barry has outdone himself."

"I know, and he must've noticed the extra locks I put on the door because he installed some as well."

Neal turned around and assessed the two extra locks on the door before he turned to her with a wry smile. "I guess this means you're moving out?"

Delta walked into his waiting arms and breathed in his scent. "Well I do first need to get furniture, and that might take quite some time."

"True, furniture can take a long time. Especially if you're looking for the right pieces."

Delta laughed as Neal bent down and kissed her. Maybe a new

apartment was necessary to start her new life.

"You bought me a pen," Neal said against her hair.

"To say thank you for taking in a stray."

Neal laughed before kissing her. "It reminds me of your eyes."

"I bought it because it reminded me of your eyes," Delta said, pulling back and looking into his blue eyes.

"The green swirls are yours, so I guess it's a little of both our eyes."

Delta looked at the pen he held in his hand and smiled. He was right, the pen represented them both. The perfect gift to remind him of their time together when it finally came to an end.

"Girl! That sounds wonderful. So when are you moving back in?" Nadine asked.

Delta had the phone balanced between her shoulder and her ear as she struggled with the bags in her hands. She had spent the afternoon shopping for her new apartment and making a decent dent in her savings account.

"Well, we're going furniture shopping this weekend, so I'll see how it goes," Delta said as her apartment building came into sight.

The evening commuters had just started going home, and the street was teeming with cars beside her. She wondered what time Neal would be home. "Although I did some shopping this morning, and I must say, Nadine, I got the most beautiful wine glasses."

"We'll have to try them out some time." Nadine laughed.

"Yes. We should."

"So how are things with Neal?"

Delta bit her lip, thinking of an easy answer, but it wasn't easy. They had agreed they were just friends with benefits, but Delta couldn't imagine not having Neal in her life. In such a short time, he had inched his way into her life and her heart, and she wasn't ready to acknowledge either yet. "Neal's fine."

"Still just friends?" Nadine purred.

"Nadine, I told you things have changed. We're friends with benefits."

"It's only a matter of time before you need to face your feelings for him, sweetheart," Nadine said kindly.

Delta sighed as she stopped in front of her building. "I know, Nadine, but I'm not ready yet. And besides, I don't even know if Neal is looking for a relationship."

"Honey, you won't know if you won't ask, and you won't ask

while you're still scared."

"I'm not scared," Delta said defiantly.

"This morning when you went shopping, how many times did you look over your shoulder?"

Delta wanted to deny looking over her shoulder, but she could be honest with Nadine. "Fine, a few times. But really, I'm doing better. I even hugged my landlord."

Both women burst out laughing. "Progress!" Nadine said triumphantly. "Well, I'll let you go make some more progress; I'm heading to the diner."

"Thanks, Nadine."

"For what?" Nadine asked, confused.

"For being my friend."

"Ha! I should thank you. Most women hate me because I'm black and beautiful."

Delta laughed before hanging up. She waved at the doorman as she stepped into the elevator, thinking of Nadine's words. The time would come when she and Neal would need to discuss their feelings, but Delta wasn't ready yet. Especially if Neal didn't feel the same way she did.

Delta walked to Neal's apartment door out of habit before

turning around and walking across the hall to her own. It would be better to store all the new items for her apartment there. She unlocked the door and pushed it open with her shoulder. She was walking inside and placing the bags carefully on the kitchen island when she heard the door click closed behind her.

She didn't need to turn to know who it was. The stench of whisky and sweat surrounded her as the hairs on the back of her neck raised. Delta searched in her vicinity for anything that could work as a weapon, but the only thing that was close enough was her keys.

Without turning around, she took a deep breath and spoke softly. "I'm waiting for the police to meet me here about the arson investigation."

"Bullshit! They've cleared you, written the whole thing off as some nuisance teenagers."

"How do you…" Delta asked, feeling panic rise and her knees weakening with fear.

"The guy I hired to do it knows people; he had to make sure he was in the clear," Craig's voice slurred, and Delta knew he had a few drinks before finding her. She closed her eyes and searched for the hate and anger she had buried for so long before she whipped around. "The guy you hired? Are you saying you did this?"

In the months Delta had been gone, he had gained weight. The buttons of his shirt were bulging, and his shirt was stretched tightly over his abdomen.

"I didn't do it; I hired someone to do it. Although he screwed it up, still need to talk to him about that." He scratched his chin that was covered with at least three days' worth of growth. "He was supposed to do it good and proper so you were framed and discredited as a firefighter."

The evil motivation behind his actions infuriated Delta. "You asshole, you couldn't even do that right."

"That's why I'm here to teach you a lesson," Craig said, moving forward. "Then I'm taking you home."

"Craig, I'm not scared of you anymore," Delta said, lifting her chin defiantly even though her heart was hammering against her chest as fear pounded through her body.

His hand closed around her upper arm like a vice, and with a swift tug, he threw Delta across the open space. Her wind got knocked out as she hit the floor, but she knew there wasn't time to catch it.

She cowered into a corner as Craig closed in on her, that menacing grin splitting his face in two. Last time, she crawled out of their apartment, bloody and beaten.

Delta had a feeling there would be no crawling out today as Craig's shadow fell over her.

Chapter 21

NEAL LEFT THE office early. Not because he didn't have work to do but because he wanted to cherish every minute he had with Delta before she moved out, and he knew that would be soon.

He also knew they would need to have a conversation about their relationship. Even though they had agreed to be friends with benefits, Neal realized it had grown into something more important.

He wasn't looking forward to the conversation either. In the past, he had avoided any conversations relating to relationships and the future, but with Delta he knew he needed to open up if he wanted to keep her in his life. Another thing he needed to deal with. Neal had never envisioned the house with the picket fence and 2.5 children with the perfect wife. For him, the future had always held justice, consisting of spending hours over case files and even longer ones in a courtroom.

Delta had changed that.

Ever since he had gotten to know her better, Neal had subconsciously gained a balance between his work life and home life. It wasn't a perfectly balanced scale and probably never would be, but it was a giant step up from where he was a few months ago.

He wanted to tell Delta how he felt, but first he needed to figure it out for himself. Was the thing between them just a passing infatuation, or did he want to keep her in his life? Both questions Neal hadn't had the courage to answer for himself.

When he did, he wanted to make sure the answers were what he wanted for the long haul. Not an easy equation for someone who had never considered someone else in the long term.

He stopped in front of the apartment building and glanced up towards his own apartment, wondering what Delta was doing. She would be off today, and if he judged by her usual routine, she would be cooking up a storm or sleeping on the couch. He would feel welcomed by both.

Without a thought, he took the elevator, grateful his brief elevator-fear had passed, and thought about the weekend ahead. Delta wanted him to go furniture shopping with her, when in fact he didn't want her to move out. He understood her need for independence, but why go back if they were moving forward? That was the crux of the matter, wasn't it? They hadn't spoken about moving forward.

The elevator doors opened, and Neal stepped out. He was wondering what type of furniture she was looking for when he heard the thud. He stood still, narrowed his eyes, and listened again. It wasn't coming from the apartments close to the elevator, so he moved forward a few steps and stood quietly to listen.

Thud!

The noise was coming from Delta's apartment. Uneasiness scratched at Neal's sixth sense as he walked towards her door. He heard a man's voice slurring, followed by another thump.

Without second thought, Neal opened the door and walked inside to find a man towering over Delta, who was cowering in the corner like an injured animal. The man was focused on Delta, and Delta was covering her eyes. Neither of them noticed his entrance.

He was taller than Neal and heavier, but Neal could smell the stench of alcohol. He would just have to be faster. Neal realized he was looking at Craig Swift.

As Craig raised his arm to strike Delta, Neal flew across the room and grabbed his arm by the wrist before twisting it behind his back.

"What the…" Craig slurred, swinging around, ready to punch whomever had interfered.

Neal was faster. His knuckles crunched against jawbone as he landed the first blow. Craig staggered back a few steps before coming for him again.

"I suggest you step back, Mr. Swift," Neal said with a voice he normally used when addressing suspects in the witness stand.

Craig grinned at him malevolently before charging. Neal squared his shoulders and knew what he had to do. This time when his fist connected Craig's face, it was his nose that snapped. Neal briefly noticed the blood on his hand and Craig falling to the floor with a string of curses before he rushed over to Delta.

"Are you okay? Did he hurt you?" Neal said, brushing hair from her face. Her eyes were wide with fear, and the red mark from Craig's fist bloomed on her cheek.

"I'm fine," Delta said on a quivering breath.

"Give me a minute," Neal said to her as he pulled out his phone. "DA Sullivan. I need a squad car to the apartment across from mine immediately for an assault on Miss Delta Eckhart. The assailant is still on the scene, and I'll keep him here until you get here." He rambled off the address and waited for confirmation from the operator.

"I'll have squad car there in five minutes," came the curt reply.

Neal slipped his phone back into his pocket before he walked over to Craig, who was sitting on the floor as blood spurted from his nose. "That was the last time you touch her, do you understand?"

"You can't stop me, she's my girl."

"That's where you're wrong. She's my girl now." Neal spoke the words before thinking, and as soon as they were out, he knew they were the truth. Delta was his, and he didn't want to let her go. He wanted to protect her and to share his life with her. Ignoring Craig, he walked over to Delta and without asking, scooped her up into his arms. Neal briefly felt her stiffen against him.

"It's all right, you're safe now," Neal whispered against her ear.

"You're wrong; I won't stop until she's back home or dead," Craig slurred in their direction.

Neal turned around to look at the pathetic man and was just about to put Delta down to shut him up when a police officer walked in. "Mr. Sullivan?"

"That man, Craig Swift, assaulted Miss Eckhart in her own home. He has an abusive history and is being investigated for bribing police officers. You can take him in, we're making a case."

The police officer nodded before he and his partner walked over to Craig and handcuffed him. Neal didn't wait for them to escort Craig out of Delta's apartment; instead, he walked across the hall to his own, where he sat down on the couch with Delta still in his arms.

Her body was stiff against his as Neal starting running a hand over her back in a soothing manner.

"You're safe now," he repeated as his hand trailed up and down her back.

Neal felt her shoulders start to shake and for a moment thought she had a serious head injury, until he realized she was crying.

He didn't say anything; she needed to cry. She needed to let out the emotions before Neal could talk to her. For almost ten minutes, Neal held onto her as she sobbed against his chest. Her hand had fisted his tie, and the other held onto him as if he were going to disappear. By the time the tears had subsided to a mere sniffle, Neal gently lifted her chin with his finger. "He really did a number on your cheek; we need to get you cleaned up."

Delta sniffed as her green eyes looked to him for comfort. Neal gently hugged her before standing up with her still in his arms and walking to the bathroom. He set her down on the side of the bath and opened the faucets. After pouring in a generous amount of bubble bath, he dampened a face cloth before rubbing it over her tear-stained cheeks to reveal the nasty bruise underneath.

Once the bath was filled to the brim, Neal helped her undress and get into the bath. "I'm not leaving you; I'm just going to fetch us both a glass of wine. I think we need it."

Delta nodded. Only her head was visible over the dense bubbles covering her body. Neal didn't want to leave her, but knew he needed to make a call.

A few minutes later, he returned feeling better. He had pushed through a restraining order that would be effective come morning, and Craig Swift was behind bars for twenty-four hours, or until Delta made a case. Delta's eyes were closed, but Neal knew she wasn't sleeping.

"Wine?"

Delta smiled and slowly sat up. Neal noticed the flinch as she moved. "Are you hurt anywhere else?"

She shook her head. "I think my body's just in shock. It aches everywhere."

Neal was certain Delta hadn't carefully gotten to the corner he found her in, but now wasn't the time to press for details about what happened. He took a sip from his own glass and undressed, keeping his eyes on Delta. He should've given Craig a better beating for the look he had put back in Delta's eyes.

"Move a little forward," Neal said softly, as Delta watched him with wide, frightened eyes.

"You know I'm not going to hurt you, and right now I need to hold you, so scoot over."

A faint smile touched her lips as she moved forward. Neal climbed in behind her and sank down in the bath before pulling Delta back, allowing her head to rest against his chest. He ran his fingers through her hair as his other hand reached for his wine.

"We need to go to the hospital tomorrow morning so that a doctor can take a look at you and write up a report, but first you need some rest."

Delta nodded without looking. "Thank you."

Anger rushed through Neal at her words. "Don't thank me. I

was too late to stop him from touching you. He hurt you."

"If you hadn't come, I'm not sure I would still be alive." Her voice was soft as she spoke.

"I have a restraining order that will be pushed through in the morning, and then we'll make a case against him."

"Thank you for that."

"Dammit, Delta, stop thanking me. He wasn't supposed to hurt you in the first place." Neal sighed and decided to come clear. "I had someone watching him until two days ago. They were certain he wasn't going to come looking for you. They were wrong."

"Neal, none of this is your fault."

"It won't happen again," Neal said before pressing a kiss against her hair. "I won't let him touch you again."

"Because I'm your girl?" Delta asked with a hint of teasing in her voice.

Neal smiled behind her. "Exactly, because you're my girl."

"I thought we were just friends?" Delta asked, turning her head to look at him.

Her eyes were bright from crying, but the question in them was serious. Neal knew how he answered her now would determine how the conversation would go when they finally had it.

"Sometimes, certain friends come to mean more than other friends."

Delta smiled at him and leaned back against his chest. Neal put down his glass and picked up the liquid soap. After squirting a generous amount into his hand, he started leisurely rubbing it along her skin. He avoided her private parts and instead focused on her arms, legs, and back. She didn't need anyone groping her after what had just happened; tonight, she just needed a friend.

Delta sighed at his touch, and Neal knew there was no longer a decision to make. It had already been made; he would do anything in his power to keep Delta in his life. He wasn't letting her go.

Chapter 22

DELTA SNUGGLED AGAINST Neal, her back to his chest, feeling drowsy. They had sat in the bath until the water had gone cold.

Neal had helped her out and dried her off before carrying her to bed. When he had offered her food, she simply shook her head and asked him to join her. She just wanted to fall asleep and forget about seeing Craig earlier.

Neal's arm sneaked across her waist and pulled her tight against him. For a moment, Delta stiffened. She didn't have the energy or the inclination to make love tonight. She had come such a long way recovering from her fear of men, and at the moment, if felt like she was back to getting on the bus in Chicago. She knew Neal wouldn't hurt her, but that didn't mean the fear of his touch could just be pushed aside.

She was still wrapping her head around Craig's words; he had paid someone to start the fire in her apartment. Delta had known he would be vindictive for her leaving him; she just never realized the extent to which he would go. She started mentally making a list of everything she needed to do in the morning.

First, she needed to go to the doctor, then she needed to go to the police station, and after that, she needed to contact the arson investigator. Then she needed to phone the chief. No, maybe she needed to phone the chief first. Sleep gradually seeped through the worry and planning, and within minutes, Delta was breathing deeply, not aware of Neal lying wide awake and watching her with worry etched on his face.

Delta opened her eyes, knowing something was wrong. The bed was empty beside her, the sheets cold where Neal should've been. Fear trickled down her spine when she noticed the dark figure standing at the foot of the bed.

"Hello, Delta." She recognized Craig's voice and knew she needed to get away. He was blocking the door, so that wouldn't be an option.

Delta remembered the old cane that Neal had under his bed; she still wanted to ask him what is was for but hadn't gotten around to it. She jumped of the bed and was reaching under it when Craig's hand grabbed her head and slammed it against the side table.

The world went black for a second as pain tore a burning path through her head. She felt the hot liquid seeping from her forehead where it was knocked open.

Slowly, she opened her eyes, trying to focus, but it was hard through the pain and tears in her eyes. She was struggling to get her focus right when she felt the first kick. Adrenaline quickly cleared the fog from her mind as she focused on the man in front of her.

Craig was standing over her. Malice shone in his eyes as he kicked her over and over again. It hurt to breath. This time, she was sure he done more than just crack her ribs. He bent over her with his whiskey breath and whispered in her ear, "Lover boy isn't here to protect you now, is he?"

Delta felt her consciousness hanging on by a thread as Craig fisted his hand and brought it down hard on her eye socket. She gathered all her strength and shouted, hoping someone would hear her. "Help! Help!"

Craig's fist came down even harder, and Delta knew there would be no help. Silent tears slid down her cheek as she accepted her fate. Craig would kill her tonight.

Suddenly his voice was kind. "Delta. Open your eyes honey. Delta."

Delta shook her head, knowing it was a trick; he was just going to hurt her more. "No." She sobbed, hoping she could lose consciousness and forget about the pain when she was picked up from the cold floor.

"Delta, snap out of it, goddammit!" His voice was different, kind but impatient. Her head was throbbing and her lungs burning, but she refused to succumb to his coaxing.

"Delta!" His loud voice startled her, and her eyes flew open. Her eyes flitted back and forth in the room, feeling confused.

"It's okay, baby, I'm here. It was just a dream," the voice said.

Delta found her strength and scampered out of his arms, watching him. Slowly, reality started to push the sleepy haze away. Neal was holding up his hands. Even though she could see anger in his eyes, she saw concern as well.

"It was just a dream, Delta. I've been trying to wake you for about five minutes. You're safe. Craig's in a cell, and I won't let that son of a bitch ever touch you again."

Delta's breathing started coming in fast pants as stars began dancing in front of her eyes.

"Dammit, Delta, don't faint on me. Look at me, Delta." Neal's voice grew louder, loud enough to make Delta listen.

"Look at me, listen to my voice. It was just a dream, you're safe. Look at me, I won't hurt you. I need you to slow down."

Delta tried to control her breathing, but she couldn't get enough air into her lungs. When Neal's arms came around her, she tried to fight him off, but he was stronger.

He pulled her onto his lap, holding her close and whispering in her ear, "It's all right, you're all right. Just breathe."

He repeated the words enough times for Delta to start believing them. Finally the world stopped spinning, and her breathing equalized. She brushed furiously at her wet cheeks before looking at Neal. It struck her like lightning in the middle of the desert. His arms were tightly wrapped around her, but Delta knew they would never touch her with anger. His clear blue eyes were teary as he looked at her, and Delta knew why. He cared.

Neal cared for her enough to coax her out of a nightmare, to calm her, to hold her, and to be patient enough to wait until the fog cleared. Delta didn't know if it was his patience, his anger at Craig, or the care that shone in her eyes, but she knew she loved Neal. She had fallen in love unwittingly, quickly and deeply, with the man holding her. Deep down, she knew Neal didn't want a relationship, and it would hurt when he finally ended their '"friendship," but tonight, she would show him how she felt.

She ran her hand over the planes of his cheek and jaw, wanting to savor every touch.

"You scared me; I didn't know what to do." His voice sounded lost as he placed his hand over hers.

"You did exactly what I needed you to," Delta said, not knowing where the calmness in her voice came from. She looked into Neal's eyes and knew she would never be afraid of him again.

She gently pressed her lips against his; wanting to show him how much she loved him.

"Go back to sleep, you're hurt." His words were kind, but Delta ignored them.

"I want you," she breathed in a whisper as she moved in his lap until she was straddling him.

Delta could see the conflicting emotions in his eyes. He

wanted to protect her but she also noticed the hunger. The desire that turned his eyes a darker shade of blue.

Without waiting for his assent, she pulled the t-shirt he had dressed her in after their bath over her head and circled her arms around his neck. She kissed him with a fervor she didn't know she possessed, with a hunger she had never felt before, knowing that soon he would be moving on, and she would be left to pick up the pieces of her broken heart. But tonight, it was still whole, whole enough to portray her love for him.

The following morning was a mad rush. After the doctor prodded and poked at her, he asked her millions of questions in regards to past injuries. She had agreed to have scans taken of almost her entire body to back up the report with evidence of physical abuse.

Neal had taken the day off and was by her side every step of the way. At the police station, they were helped within minutes of arriving, Neal's reputation speeding the entire process up. The female police officer that took her statement was kind and thorough, and Delta had to push down the tears that threatened to fall a few times. Neal's hand held hers tight as she relived her three years with Craig, and his abuse, for the report.

Chief Kays had been kind and asked her to take as much time as she needed, but Delta had insisted on returning to the firehouse next shift. The realization that she was in love with Neal was confirmed throughout the day as he stood by her side and fought for her as they made the case against Craig. Because Neal had arrived early enough to stop Craig from doing worse damage, they could only lay a charge for breaking and entering and assault. Bail was posted by one of his lawyer friends late afternoon, but not before Neal had ensured the restraining order was in place.

Delta felt safer for it, even though she knew a piece of paper wouldn't keep Craig from touching her again. When they had gotten home early evening, Neal poured them each a glass of wine before they sat down in the living room.

"Would you like me to order in?" Neal asked, holding Delta's hand in his lap.

"I think I'd rather try to burn some food and take my mind off today," Delta said with a weak smile.

Neal laughed. "I don't mind burned food. Would you mind if I just checked my mail quickly?"

There it was, Delta thought. Her issues and her presence were already starting to interfere with his work. She considered going across the hallway and spending some time in her own empty apartment but couldn't summon the courage to do it alone. She needed to start weaning herself off Neal, and the only way was putting some space between them.

On impulse, she took her phone and texted Nadine. Within seconds, she received a reply. Delta turned to Neal, summoning her best smile, which wasn't easy, as she knew this was the first step in saving her from heartbreak.

"You know what? Why don't you catch up with your emails, and I'll head across the hall and figure out what I need for my apartment."

"Delta, I can leave the emails," Neal said, even though Delta knew he couldn't.

She stroked the day's worth of stubble on his chin. "I'll be fine. Nadine's coming over; we'll open a bottle of wine and have some girl time."

Delta noticed Neal visibly relaxing. "That's nice. Why don't I order in? Then you don't have to burn food. You can just sit back and drink wine with your friend."

Delta had mentioned Nadine a few times to Neal, and Neal

knew she was part of the abused women's group she had joined. Smiling, she stood up. "I might have a little too much wine tonight," she said, not mentioning it would be over moving away from Neal inch by inch and not over Craig.

Neal laughed. "An even better idea."

Within an hour, Delta and Nadine were sitting on lawn chairs Delta had stored in the spare room cupboard that had miraculously survived the fire, with a glass of wine each.

"I take it Neal didn't put that bruise on your cheek?" Nadine said without preamble.

"No, he didn't. Craig paid me a visit."

Nadine sat up, anger glistening in her dark brown eyes. "He didn't!"

"Yes, he did last night."

"Did you invite me over so I can drag it out of you, or are you going to tell me?"

Delta laughed and smiled at her friend. Nadine was exactly what she needed tonight, although her heart was across the hall with the blue-eyed man that had stolen it.

"I'm very good at dragging, I should just tell you that first."

"No need to drag. I think it might be good to talk about it."

"Good, so talk," Nadine said sitting up straight and putting her wine glass down.

Delta took a deep breath and repeated what had happened the night before for what felt like the millionth time that day.

Chapter 23

"GOOD MORNING," NEAL said as he pushed open Delta's bedroom door with a cup of coffee in his hand.

"Hi," Delta said, tying her hair. "Thanks for the coffee, but I'm running late," Delta answered stiffly.

"I'll put it in a thermos for you." Neal was just through the door when he turned back. "Why did you sleep here last night?" He knew his voice held a certain pathetic note to it, but he needed to know what was going on.

Ever since the first night they had made love, Delta had shared his bed. Last night she had gone to bed with him, but this morning Neal had awoken alone. Something was going on.

Delta shrugged and pulled on a light sweater. "I was tossing all night and didn't want to wake you."

Neal nodded, even though he knew she was lying. Sure, she

was tossing, but she couldn't look him in the eye. "All right. Well, I'll put this in a thermos, and when you get back tomorrow morning, we can maybe go look at some furniture."

"Actually, about that - I'm not sure tomorrow is going to work after all. I have a few errands to run."

Neal frowned and watched as Delta picked up her keys and her bag.

She followed Neal into the kitchen and watched as he poured the coffee into the traveling mug. "Bye, see you tomorrow." Her greeting sounded cheerful, but it was forced. She had barely looked at him all morning, but there wasn't time now to dig beneath the surface.

"Be safe," Neal said as she opened the front door and slipped out.

Since Craig had made his return into Delta's life, Neal sensed something was different. He wasn't sure if she was just shaken up by what happened, having old scars scratched open, or if it was something else. But Delta wasn't being herself. She rarely teased him, barely spoke, and only made eye contact when it was really necessary.

If Neal didn't know any better, he could've sworn she was

pulling away from him. The question was why?

Craig's return had made Neal realize how much Delta meant to him, how much he wanted to keep her in his life, to share a future with her. But with Delta pulling away inch by inch, Neal was lost. He had never been in this situation before and didn't know how he was going to get out of it.

He knew he had to talk to her, but she would be on shift for the next twenty-four hours, so he just needed to keep himself occupied until then.

The bar was buzzing with activity. It was Friday night, and happy hour was in full swing at the bar close to dock where Max kept his boats. The air carried salt and the scent of fried chips.

Neal grabbed a table on the deck overlooking the water and ordered two beers. Since he'd been stuck in his head all day circling around the Delta issue, Neal didn't feel like staying home tonight. He wouldn't get any work done anyway. So he had decided to meet Max for drinks.

Normally, he would go by his parents' if he had something on his mind, but he didn't have something on his mind, more like someone. His mother would try to pry it out of him in a few looks, and his father would think of solutions. Neal wasn't ready to face either.

Instead, he planned on having a few drinks with his baby brother and hopefully forgetting about Delta for a short while.

He noticed Max pushing through the crowd to reach him. His hair was windblown and his smile carefree as he sat down. "So are we having beer?"

"Already ordered," Neal said, shaking his brother's hand before they both sat down.

"It's a nice day, isn't it?" Max said, even though the wind was tossing his hair in his eyes.

"Little windy," Neal grunted.

"Nothing like the wind in your hair to make you feel alive."

Neal laughed at the words and wondered why he couldn't be more like Max. He looked at a seagull sweeping low over the water and thought about Delta. The whole point of coming out tonight was not to think about her, but everything reminded him of her.

"Earth to Neal," Max teased from across the table.

"I'm here," Neal said, rubbing is thumb over the condensation on the side of the glass.

"Yes you're here, but your head isn't. And since you never invite me for a drink, you're either looking for mind numbing conversation or you need to talk to me about something."

"I don't need to talk to you about something," Neal huffed.

"Right, so mind numbing conversation it is." Max laughed and sipped from his beer. "Have you heard from Caleb lately?"

Neal nodded. "Yeah, I spoke to him earlier this week. Apparently Sarah's only got about eight weeks left. According to Caleb, she's glowing, but apparently she's tired and uncomfortable and her feet have swollen to the size of miniature boulders."

"Sounds about right." Max nodded.

"What do you know about pregnancy?" Neal asked, drawing his eyebrows together.

"Apparently more than you, but that might change soon," Max teased, winking at Neal.

Neal nearly sputtered his beer over the table. "What the hell do you mean?"

Max laughed robustly, and Neal noticed a couple of girls glance his way at the sound. His brother had always been a magnet to the fairer sex. "I just mean that Delta is a great girl, and it seems to me like you're whipped."

"I'm not whipped," Neal said determinedly.

Max leaned forward, smiling. "Fine, maybe the term 'whipped' is a little high school. How about, you seem in love?"

Neal started to argue but knew it wouldn't be worth the waste of air. Max was right. "Fine, and if I was, hypothetically, what would I do about it?"

"Seems to me Delta's a little complicated? You sure you want to go there with her?" Max asked carefully.

Anger bubbled up even as Neal's hand clenched around the beer. "Mom told you, didn't she?"

Max held up his hands. "Mom told me nothing. I have eyes in my head and a fair amount of experience with women. She jumped when I touched her, and she has shadows in her eyes."

Neal frowned, leaning forward on his arms and seeing his brother in a new light. Maybe Max had grown up after all. "Since you're being so adult and insightful, I'll give it to you."

"Oh, so you do want to talk?" At Neal's murderous glance, Max held up his hands. "I'm listening."

The waitress brought their second round of beers and left them but after ogling at Max for about thirty seconds straight.

"Delta's previous boyfriend had itching fists and twitching palms. That's why she came to Wilmington. He showed up about a week ago from Chicago and smacked her around again."

"Shit. Is she alright?" Max sighed.

"Yeah, well except for the bruise on her cheek, the doc said she's fine, but something's off."

"Like what?"

"Since then she's been pulling away. I know I should be glad she's the one pulling away as it's normally me, but what if I don't want her to?"

"You mean you'd like her to stick around and find out what's between you?" Max asked, frowning.

"Max, don't give me shit. I like her, and I've already screwed this up by agreeing to only be friends with benefits."

"Oh boy, I didn't take you for the friends with benefits type." Max laughed.

Neal was reaching for his keys when Max's hand closed over his. "Listen, I'm kidding. From where I'm sitting, it seems to me you've only got one option."

"Oh, and what's that?" Neal asked irritably.

Max's eyes were serious when he spoke again. None of the

normal teasing and lightheartedness shone in them, only genuine concern. "If you want her to stick around, you need to decide what you mean by that. Are you looking at a relationship or something more long term?"

"And if I'm not sure?" Neal asked.

"You need to be sure. You need to face your feelings, and then you need to lay them on the table and let her decide."

Neal sighed. "I know, but that's not an easy ask. I'm not good with feelings."

"Sounds to me like you want to ask this girl to share the rest of your life with you. Considering that, it's not that big an ask."

"Fair enough," Neal answered, knowing his baby brother was right. If he wanted to stop Delta from pulling away even further, he would need to tell her how he felt about her.

"And you need to do something about the ex," Max said.

"Already on it. We've charged him breaking and entering and laid an assault charge. I've also gotten a restraining order against him."

"Neal, if that guy came all this way to find her, do you really think a piece of paper is going to stop him?"

Neal shrugged, because Max had just said what he'd been

thinking all along.

Feeling worried, he pulled out his phone and texted Delta.

Hope you're saving lives and staying safe.

Can we talk tomorrow?

Neal

Max leaned over and laughed. "You think that'll give you enough time to sort through your own laundry basket of mixed emotions?"

Before Neal could answer Max, his phone beeped.

Shift's quiet, reading a book.

Talk tomorrow.

D

Neal smiled at the message before handing the phone to Max. "Now I have to do the laundry before tomorrow morning at seven."

Max laughed. "Want another beer?"

Neal glanced at his own empty glass before smiling at Max. "I don't, but that girl with red hair has been watching you for ten minutes. I think she'd like one."

Both men laughed before bidding their goodbyes with a slap and a hug.

Neal stepped into the quiet apartment a short while later and made himself a cup of tea. He had a lot of thinking to do tonight and wasn't sure he was ready for it. He had never planned for the long term with anybody, but Max was right. If he didn't decide how he was going to approach this with Delta, he might just lose her.

By seven the next morning, Neal had a pretty clear idea of what he wanted to say to Delta. He had barely slept, spending most of the night watching reruns of *Criminal Minds* and thinking about her. She was due home any minute. Neal had already showered and made her a farmhouse breakfast. Freshly squeezed orange juice was placed on the dining room table, ready for their talk.

He knew it might be a bit over the top, but this morning was special. Neal had just about gotten everything ready when his phone beeped. He opened the message and felt his world drop away.

Chapter 24

WHAT DID NEAL want to talk about, Delta wondered as she walked home after her shift. It was a cool morning with a hint of mist that Mike had promised would reveal a beautiful sunny day.

Ever since Neal's text last night, a feeling of dread had settled over Delta. She had a good suspicion of what Neal wanted to talk to her about.

He wanted her to move out; their fling was over. He was an attractive man and probably had another "friend" lined up already. Delta had been preparing herself for this since the night she realized she was in love with Neal, but still, no preparation could prepare her heart to be broken.

Her usual brisk pace was more leisurely this morning. It was Saturday, and she and Neal would've gone to look at furniture for her apartment today. Instead, she was being dumped.

Emotion clogged her throat, but she swallowed it down. What did she expect? Did she really think Neal Sullivan was going to be her happily ever after? Men like Neal don't ever settle down. He'll always be chasing the law, and the law would always come first.

Once she and Neal had had their talk, Delta decided she would go to the second hand furniture shop in Wrightsville Beach alone. The last time she had been there, they had beautiful pre-loved pieces she would love to have in her apartment. The kind of pieces you keep for a lifetime, not just a fashion statement. After Neal broke up with her, the last thing she wanted to do was spend the day in his apartment. She would get what she needed in Wrightsville Beach and pay extra for them to deliver today. Tonight, she would be sleeping in her own apartment.

She would've loved it if Neal would have come with her. They could've made a day of it: gone somewhere for lunch afterwards, and spent the afternoon walking on the beach hand in hand. Delta had just rounded the corner to their apartment when an arm slipped around her waist.

"Hello there, gorgeous. Time to come home," Craig whispered against her ear.

Delta was struggling to get free when she felt her whole body spasm uncontrollably and the world went black.

Craig smiled as an old lady walked by, frowning at Delta unconscious in his arms. "It's my wife, she's been fainting ever since she got pregnant." He gave the old lady a charming grin before slipping his one hand under her knees and picking her up.

Today he would teach her a lesson, a lesson that would stay with her forever. No one walks out on Craig Swift. Who the hell did she think she was? Disappearing like that. Leaving him to answer to her friends, her boss, hell, even his family. It had been embarrassing to say the least. Sure, most of them bought the story that she had gone to travel Europe, but that had all fallen apart when her chief called him to ask for Delta's current address. He needed a place to send her letter of recommendation, and Craig's number was listed as her next of kin.

She wouldn't make that mistake again. He carried her into the alley where he had parked his rented car and pressed a button to open the trunk.

Delta started moving in his arms just as he set her down in the trunk. He smiled at her malevolently. "We're going for a little ride,

Delta. Then I'm going to teach you a lesson."

He slammed the trunk of the car just as she started kicking and screaming, music to his ears. Craig whistled as he moved around the car and slid behind the wheel. His palms had been twitching for months on end, and the other night had just whet his appetite when her prosecutor boyfriend had rushed in.

Oh yes, he knew all about her prosecutor boyfriend. He had found Delta a few months after she had left Chicago but was sure she would return. When she didn't come back and Terry screwed up the arson setup, he knew he had to take care of his own business.

When he was done with her today, she would never run from him again. Delta's muffled screams sounded through the car, and Craig switched on the radio just as "Bad Moon Rising" started playing.

Craig cheerfully whistled along; he was really looking forward to today.

When she realized her screams wouldn't be heard over the music, Delta kept quiet. Her mind was foggy as she blinked in the dark. She knew she was in a trunk, and she knew Craig had put her there. Other than that she had no idea what just happened. One moment she was walking down the street, and the next she was in the trunk of a car.

Delta pinched her eyes shut and thought back to the exact sequence of events. He Tased her, she realized as she tried moving her arms and legs. Her whole body was sore, as if she had done a full day of training the day before. She groped around in the dark for her bag, but it wasn't there.

Tears threatened to fall when she remembered Craig's words; he was going to teach her a lesson. Delta tried to shift onto her side and was feeling something sticking into her side when she realized what it was. She slowly unzipped the side pocket of her coat and pulled out her phone. Her battery was still full, but Delta knew Craig would take it once they stopped, and that could be any minute.

She quickly swiped the screen and typed a text to Neal, hoping he would read it.

Craig.

In car.

Track my phone.

Hurry.

After making sure the message went through, Delta turned her phone on silent and prayed to the heavens that Neal had received the message. After what felt like a forever to Delta, although it was more like twenty minutes, the car stopped. She quickly switched on her phone and found a message from Neal.

I'm on my way.

It was sent two minutes ago; she just had to hold on long enough for Neal to get to her, Delta thought as she switched off the phone and put it back in her pocket.

Craig's grin was charming when he opened the trunk. "You're looking good. Your physicality probably lessened the blow from the Taser gun."

Delta seethed with anger, but she kept quiet. Once he got her out of the car, she would run.

Craig leaned forward and was taking her hand to help her out of the trunk when Delta tried to shove her fingers in his eyes.

She heard him curse and felt the blow almost simultaneously. Darkness surrounded her once more as she was carried into a dingy motel room just off the highway. Her arms flailed as Craig tossed her onto the bed. He tied both her arms behind her back before securing her feet.

Light flickered through her eyelids, and slowly she came to. She tugged at the rope on her arms and legs, wincing at the throbbing pain behind her eye. *That wasn't a warning shot*, Delta thought as she spotted Craig across the room with a bottle of whiskey. Fear pumped through her veins as she realized she wouldn't be dumped today after all; she would be killed.

Chapter 25

NEAL BLINKED A few times as his breathing quickened. Delta wouldn't have sent a message like that on a whim. Craig had her, and whatever he planned on doing with Delta wouldn't be good.

He quickly dialed one of his informers. "I need you to track a cellphone signal, Terry."

"That's against the law, Mr. Prosecutor."

"Listen you shit, I can have it done by the cops, but I need a location within a few minutes. Can you help me or not?"

There was silence on the end of the line for a few seconds before the guy grunted, "Fine, give me the number."

Neal rattled off the number before putting down the phone. He dialed 911 next and relayed the situation to them. "I'm sorry, sir, but we need to have a location to be able to help. And since it's only been a few hours, she's not really missing yet."

Neal clenched his teeth. He never threw his position in anyone's face, but this time it was different. "Listen to me closely. This is State Prosecutor Sullivan speaking. My girlfriend has a restraining order against her abusive ex-boyfriend." He rattled off names and social security numbers before taking a breath. "She was supposed to meet me this morning just after seven but instead sent me a text message saying Craig had put her in the trunk of his car."

Neal heard the woman's fingers rapidly run over a keyboard before she spoke again. "I'm sorry, Mr. Sullivan. We'll get right on this."

"You better," Neal said before hanging up the phone and redialing Terry's number.

The phone rang a few times before Terry answered. "Just give me ten minutes. I'll get it, and just know this is going to cost you," Terry barked into the phone before hanging up on Neal.

Neal grunted and started pacing through his apartment. He knew he had to wait for Terry to get him a location, but every second was another second Craig could hurt Delta. He picked up his phone and pressed speed dial.

"Neal? Is something wrong? Why are you phoning so early?"

Susan Sullivan's voice was sleepy, and Neal knew it was no use bothering them with this.

"Hi, Mom. Don't worry about it; go back to sleep," Neal said, feeling stupid for phoning his parents in the first place.

"Neal, what's going on? You wouldn't phone me for nothing, so spit it out."

Neal felt his throat thicken as he sat down on the side of the couch. "He's got her, Mom. Her ex-boyfriend's got her. I'm just waiting for them to track her phone, then I'm going to find her."

"What? Oh my gosh, Neal, are you sure? Who's tracking the phone?" Susan said, shocked.

"A guy I know. Sorry for bothering you, I just..." Neal struggled to string the words together.

His father's voice came onto the line; his mother had obviously put him on speakerphone. "I know, son. You love her."

"Yes. I was going to tell her this morning."

"So let the police find her, and then you tell her," Susan pleaded as Neal heard an incoming call alert.

"I've got to go; I'll let you know as soon as I've got her," Neal said before hanging up and ignoring his mother's request. He pressed the answer button again.

"Terry? Where is she?" Neal barked into the phone.

"We've got her signal coming from a motel on highway 421," Terry said. "I only take cash."

"What's the address?" Neal demanded.

Terry rattled off the name of a sleazy motel Neal had driven by in the past before demanding his money again.

"Terry, I've got enough on you to put you away for a long time, but I leave you on the streets because you're a reliable informer. Would you rather do time or stay an informer?"

Neal heard Terry take a deep breath and release it. "Fine."

"Fine," Neal said before hanging up the phone. Terry had never been involved in any serious crimes, but he always knew who was involved. It was informers like Terry who showed Neal which rocks to turn to find answers that would make his criminal cases stand even with a fancy lawyer on the other side. But there was no way Neal was going to pay him for illegally tracking a cellphone.

Neal grabbed his keys and ran out the door, knowing it was only a matter of time before Craig would kill Delta. He already had a restraining order against him, and he wasn't going to put his reputation on the line. Craig wasn't planning on letting Delta live long enough to report him violating the terms of both his bail and the restraining order.

He pulled his car out of the small parking lot with tires screeching as he phoned 911 again. After relaying the location, he switched off the phone and pressed his foot down hard on the gas. Before anything happened to Delta, he needed to tell her that he loved   her.

Chapter 26

DELTA WATCHED THE clock on the wall, counting the minutes. How long did it take to track a phone signal, she wondered as she watched Craig drink. The bottle of whiskey had already taken a decent knock, and Delta knew she would be next.

"Want a sip?" Craig slurred at her from across the room. He poured a little whiskey into a mug and bought it to Delta. He held it carefully in front of her mouth, allowing her to sip. Delta did as she was told. If she was going to be killed, she didn't want it to be painful, so she'd cooperate for as long as she could.

She had just sipped the fiery liquid down when Craig's laugh rang through the room. He quickly sobered and pulled the cup away. "You didn't think I brought you here to drink, did you?"

Delta slowly shook her head and watched as his eyes turned black. A wicked look that reminded Delta of a demon, or something equally evil, shone in his eyes as he brought his hand back. The slap hit her with such force that she was thrown off the bed. With no way to cushion the fall, she slammed into the wall, hitting her head on the side table. She heard the crunch of her telephone just as her hip landed on it.

"That's more like it," Craig sneered. "Now you wait there until I'm ready to teach you a lesson."

Delta knew something in Craig had snapped. He had hit her before, but he had never seemed to enjoy it as much as he did today. It was almost as if he was drawing it out, gaining pleasure from watching her wait in pain, with fear shining in her eyes. She had a feeling she already knew what the lesson was; she had to be dead before she left him.

He poured himself another whiskey and drank leisurely as he watched Delta across the room. His ringtone jingled, and Delta hoped he would answer it, giving her an opportunity to scream. Craig picked up the phone, looking at Delta as he answered.

"Hello, Cindy." Within two steps, Craig was standing over her with a knife against her cheek, his eyes warning her not to make a sound. "No, everything's just dandy. Yes, I met up with Delta, she's right here." Delta could hear his secretary's voice cheerfully asking him when he would be back.

Craig sneered at Delta as he answered, "I'll be back in the office by Monday. All right then, I'll make sure to bring Delta with."

He laughed as he put the phone down. "They think I'm joining you on a short holiday before we *both* return to Chicago."

Delta closed her eyes, hoping she was right to keep quiet. If Neal couldn't find her, she had just thrown her only chance of living down the drain.

It had been almost thirty minutes since they arrived. Where was Neal? Delta started planning on ways to get attention but knew that screaming wouldn't help. Craig wouldn't be stupid enough to get a room adjacent to an occupied one. Screaming would get her nowhere.

Craig swallowed down his whiskey before standing up and moving towards Delta. He unbuckled his belt and slid it out of the hoops before wrapping it around his hand. "Time for your lesson," he said as he landed the first shot.

Delta flinched and crouched against the wall as the shot landed against her back. Her wind was completely knocked out, but it would've done a lot more damage to her face.

Craig's voice slurred over her, and Delta looked up. "If you're not going to keep still, this is going to be a lot more fun than I had in mind." He unwrapped the belt around his hand, letting the buckle hang free.

Craig's arm lifted, the buckle swinging in the air, and Delta closed her eyes, knowing it would hurt a lot more than his fists.

Chapter 27

HE SLAMMED THE brakes as he pulled into a parking space, and the burning rubber left a trail of smoke in the parking lot of the motel. Neal jumped out of the car, assessing the building.

It was early spring, and he doubted the motel would be full. The reception office was on the other side of the building. Neal decided against going there first; every minute counted at this stage. He started at the last door to the left, furthest from the reception office.

If you wanted to hurt someone, that would be the best spot, Neal thought as he ran towards the door. There were a few cars parked in the parking lot, but Neal couldn't be sure which one was Craig's. He slammed on the door a few times and moved onto the next one when it didn't open.

By the fourth door, Neal was starting to doubt Terry's

information when he heard the thump followed by a crash. He moved quietly to the next door, listening closely for either Delta or Craig's voice.

"If you're not going to keep still, this is going to be a lot more fun than I had in mind." Craig's muffled slur came through the door.

Neal thought about calling the police first to find out how far out they were, but he decided against it. He gently tested the doorknob to see if it was unlocked; it wasn't.

Dragging a hand through his hair, he took a few steps backwards before taking a deep breath.

Neal ran into the door like a bull into a red flag and felt the pain spread through his shoulder as he burst into the room. Craig's eyes flitted from Delta to Neal as he swung the belt in his hand, the buckle building momentum. Neal moved forward and noticed the brief flicker of defeat in Craig's eyes before Craig turned and kicked Delta full force in the abdomen.

Something snapped. Neal wasn't sure what it was, as it had never snapped for him before, but once it did, there was no stopping him. His vision turned red, his only focus Craig, as he moved forward. Without concern for his own safety or checking to see if Craig had a firearm, Neal leaped for him, body slamming him against the floor.

Craig grinned at him smugly and turned to laugh at Delta. Neal intended to only punch him once, but as his first blow landed, he lost control. He thought of how many times that man had done it to Delta. He thought of the pain she had endured, the nightmares that still haunted her, and how her eyes still had shadows in them when she got lost in her own memories.

As his fists crushed into Craig's face again and again, Neal didn't hear Delta shouting for him to stop or even notice that Craig had stopped fighting back. He vaguely noticed the blood on his hands and the pain in his shoulder but chose to ignore it. The only thing he knew was that he was going to make Craig pay for what he did to Delta.

When Delta's hand touched his shoulder, Neal regained control. She looked at him with her big green eyes: lost, scared, and grateful. He briefly glanced at Craig, who hadn't moved, and stood up. With a quick scoop, he had Delta in his arms and carried her outside just as the police cars sped into the parking lot with alarms wailing.

Neal sat down on the short curb with Delta in his arms and

glanced at the police officer approaching them.

"He's inside; take him away before I hurt him even more," Neal said before looking at Delta.

Her one eye was swollen shut. The bruise on her jaw hadn't fully healed from the last time, and Neal was sure she would be bruised from where Craig had kicked her out of spite. Gently, he untied the rope binding her hands and feet. "I've got you, baby, you're safe now." Neal whispered against her lips before Delta pushed him away.

"I appreciate you saving me, but don't pity me. You wanted to break up with me this morning, so just get it over with. But please, I beg you, Neal - don't pretend to care when you don't." Her voice was hoarse as tears rolled over her cheeks.

Neal frowned at her, confused. "Who said I wanted to break up with you?"

"You did. Right from the start, you made it clear that whatever this was it was temporary, and clearly you want out."

Neal smiled at her before pressing a kiss against her forehead. "I think you need to look a little closer, Delta. That clearly isn't what I want. I wanted to talk to you this morning about something else."

It was Delta's turn to frown through the tears. "What? Oh, you want me to move out," she said dejectedly.

"No, Delta. I want you to stay." Neal knew the words sounded weak, but they were the most important ones he had ever spoken.

"What do you mean?" Delta asked through a fresh wave of tears.

"I want you to stay. I want to be more than your friend. I want to be your best friend, your lover, and if you don't mind the term, your boyfriend."

Delta giggled; even though her one eye was swollen shut and her cheek bruised, it was the best sound Neal had heard all morning. "So you care?"

"Yes, of course I care. Why do you think I nearly killed a man with my bare hands?" Neal said with a laugh. "How could you even think otherwise?"

"I just didn't think you'd....didn't you say the law always comes first with you?" Delta asked.

Neal understood her question; she didn't want to play second fiddle to his career. "And with you, a fire will always come first. It's who we are, it's what we do, but it doesn't mean it has to be the only thing we do. I'd like to do you too." Neal laughed at the ridiculous phrasing of his own words.

"Me too," Delta said before resting her head against his chest and sighing deeply.

EPILOGUE

"I FEEL LIKE a whale with stones for feet and a constant fire pushing its way up my throat."

"You're as pretty as a rose and just tired. Just a few more weeks, then we'll hold him in our arms."

"Easy for you to say since you're not the one that can't sleep, can't eat, and barely has any clothes that fit."

Neal laughed and turned to Delta. "I think Sarah should be bottled as a cure for broodiness, she sure makes pregnancy sound like death sentence."

Delta smiled at Sarah, who was thirty-seven weeks pregnant. "I haven't been pregnant before, but you have my sympathies. It does look uncomfortable, especially in this heat."

Delta felt Neal's hand resting on her knee and smiled at him. It was a lovely summer's day in the high nineties, and they were having a backyard barbecue at Neal's parents'. The whole family was there since Caleb and Sarah had come for a final visit before the baby came.

"Why are you so quiet today?" Max asked Delta teasingly as he refilled her glass of wine. Since Craig had been sentenced and sent to jail a few months ago, Delta had been a lot more bubbly. Her relationship with Neal was heading somewhere Delta never imagined it would, and for the first time in her life, she knew she truly loved a good and honest man.

When she didn't answer, Max slapped Caleb on the back before turning to her. "You're not still star struck over C.B. Sullivan over here, are you?"

Delta laughed. "No, although I had to force myself to leave my C.B. Sullivan collection at home." She smiled at Caleb. "I was hoping you could sign them but thought since I was only meeting you today, it could wait."

Lisa and Susan returned from the kitchen where they had just put the finishing touches on the salads when Mac spoke up. "You hear that, Suze, Delta's planning on seeing Caleb again, so I guess she's almost part of the family."

Everyone laughed, but deep down, Delta hoped that was the case. She had fallen in love completely with Neal and was starting to fall in love with his family as well.

Caleb had congratulated her on getting Neal to smile more, and Lisa had asked her if she was drugging him secretly. Apparently, Neal had never smiled as much as he had since he and Delta had officially become a couple.

Lisa had spent fifteen minutes telling Delta about her new crush. A young British student with pale skin and an exotic accent. Delta had never considered British accents to be exotic, but then, she wasn't Lisa.

"So Sarah, are both baby rooms done yet?" Lisa asked, turning to Sarah.

Delta found the story about Sarah running away from her own wedding very entertaining and still saw small things that reminded her that she was a Southern debutante, besides her Southern accent.

"Why do you need two baby rooms?" Delta asked, confused.

"They live in Blue Hill mostly but spend their winters and weekends in Wrightsville Beach," Neal said beside her.

"Just about, although we're not putting all the gadgets in Wrightsville at the moment. We'll first see what we really use."

"Sounds like a good plan," Susan said before joining her husband at the barbecue and whispering something in his ear.

Mac excused himself, and Delta turned back to Lisa and Sarah. Sitting with a glass of wine in her hand and so much love surrounding her really did her soul good. She could imagine spending holidays and special events with the people surrounding her right now, with Neal by her side. Delta was still thinking about what their first Christmas together would be like when her phone rang. She noticed Chief Kays' private number and answered swiftly after excusing herself.

"Chief?"

"I'm sorry to bother you, Delta, but Mike's fallen ill with stomach flu, and I was hoping you could cover his shift for him."

Delta sighed softly, glancing at the group of people all watching her. "Sure, Chief. I'll be there in a few."

After numerous hugs and see-you-soons were exchanged, Neal offered to drop her by the station.

A short while later, they pulled up outside, but the bay doors were closed. *Strange*, Delta thought. Bay doors were rarely closed. She got out and quickly kissed Neal goodbye and was walking towards the side door when the bay door's started to open.

For a moment, Delta thought she was hallucinating when behind the doors weren't just the usual truck and engine but bunches and bunches of flowers. She was blinking a few times to make sure her vision wasn't fooling her when her crew came out through the side door to stand by her side.

"What's going on?" Delta asked as her eyes perused the colorful daisies, irises, violets, poppies, daffodils, and a million other flowers she didn't know the names of.

"You better ask him," Mike said, pushing through the men.

"I thought you were sick?" Delta asked, confused.

Mike smiled. "Like I said, better ask him." He pointed to where Neal was leaning against his car with a wide smile.

Delta shook her head and watched him walk towards her. "What's all this?" she asked, feeling giddy.

"I know you said I'm not allowed to send flowers to the firehouse, so I didn't. I got Mike here to buy them for you."

Delta laughed, moving forward and picking up a bright pink daisy. "Why?"

Neal smiled as he took her hand. "Because I needed a way to tell you I love you that you won't ever forget." He took her hands before glancing at the crew. "And I needed an audience to put some pressure on. It's always harder to say no in front of an audience."

Delta felt butterflies swooping in circles in her abdomen. "Neal?"

Neal got down on one knee and kissed her hand. "Stay. But this time, let's make it forever?"

"Are you asking me to marry you?"

"Damn right," and "Are you deaf?" came the comments from her crew.

Delta laughed and looked at Neal. "I'm asking you to share your life with me - the good, the bad, and the ugly. And if Sarah hasn't scared you off, I'd like to have children with you as well."

Laughter bubbled from Delta as Neal spoke all the words she had hoped to hear. "Of course!"

"Great!" Neal pulled her in for a steamy kiss, earning howls from the crew and a few loud claps from Chief Kays. "There's just one catch."

"What?" Delta asked, breathless from the kiss.

"You have to love me for the rest of your life."

Delta laughed. "Done."

THE END

Did You Read Bride on the Run?

(Book 1 in the Sullivan Family Series)

A southern debutante and a writer with a Jekyll and Hyde personality, can love really overcome any obstacle?

Sarah Rothman has been leading the life of a southern debutante until her perfect world came crashing down. Running from her wedding along with her parents' expectations she finds herself in Maine.

Caleb Sullivan, renowned writer and playboy famous for his mercurial personality retreats to Maine to focus on his next bestseller.

When Sarah and Caleb meet they both insist on denying the attraction between them, each for their own reasons.
But when Sarah's life is threatened, both Caleb and Sarah are forced to acknowledge the feelings they have for each other.

Will Sarah learn to trust again? Can Caleb let go of the pain of the past and allow himself to fall in love again?

Book 1 in the Sullivan Family Series, filled with danger, deceit, and desire.

ABOUT THE AUTHOR

Milan Watson is the mother of two little boys and wife to a supportive husband, who doesn't mind doing the dishes when she finds herself lost in a story.

　She spends most of her days dreaming up new characters and bringing stories to life, surrounded by her family and her two dogs, Wendy and Kingston. She loves creating characters you can identify with and writing stories that will have you laugh, cry and smile at the same time.

You can follow her page on Facebook for new releases:
Milan Watson Author.
If you'd like to sign up for her mailing list feel free to send her a
mail at <u>milanwatsonauthor@gmail.com</u>

Did you enjoy this book? Please leave a quick review and spread the word on either Goodreads or Amazon

Would you like a free book? Sign up for my mailing list and be the first to know about new releases in the Sullivan Family Series. You can just visit www.milanwatson.com to sign up. Be the first to know about special offers and new releases.

www.ingramcontent.com/pod-product-compliance
Lightning Source LLC
Chambersburg PA
CBHW070810180626
46818CB00001B/199